THE SNOWS OF AETALUS

Distributed by:
Engen Books
www.engenbooks.com
submissions@engenbooks.com

First mass market paperback printing: March 2021

Cover Design: Ellen Curtis

Slipstreamers Committee:
Amanda Labonté
Ali House
AJ Ryan
Ellen Curtis
Erin Vance
Lauralana Dunne
Matthew LeDrew

THE SNOWS OF AETALUS

SHANNON K GREEN & JD RYOT

BOOKS

CHAPTER ONE

"Okay class, hope you all have a great break." Cassidy Cane watched her students file out of the classroom. Pulling her hair into a ponytail, she took all evidence of herself from the room and walked into the hall. Checking the notifications on her phone turned up the same old things: an email from the university, probably announcing the instructors for the next semester, including the fact that she wouldn't be one; messages from the bank, probably about late payments or the new credit card she wouldn't qualify for; and, just for something new, a missed call from her dentist. At least the last one might just be an appointment and not a bill reminder.

As she entered her office, she slipped her phone into her purse without turning the ringer back on, then sat at her desk to begin grading the first of the term papers. She took the opportunity to bask in the air conditioning as much as she could, and drank as much iced tea as she could handle in the break room before stepping into the humid June air and walking the short distance to her apartment. Once there, she plugged in her phone, setting an alarm for early the next day.

As she shrugged out of her blazer, she remembered that classes had ended for the semester but decided that going back in to grade the papers was a preferable choice to sitting in her sultry apartment alone. True, she could call somebody to hang out, but that would cost money, and money would be getting tight with no lecture position next semester and no digs scheduled for the summer. Instead, she fixed herself a light supper from what was left in the refrigerator, making herself a note reminding her that she needed to do the grocery shopping tomorrow. Then she curled up on the couch with the latest Verdant Church novel between fitful naps.

As she read, her mind began retracing her route from classroom to office, from office to her building, constructing a web of her daily movements. Everyday repeating the same paths, more or less, and soon that would be coming to an end to be replaced by something else. Something new to build a new pattern while she struggled with the same problems of being underpaid when she had work and just plain broke when she didn't. On that cheery note she decided to actually read the messages that had come through on her phone while she had been ignoring it. She saw three missed texts and two missed calls from Doctor Gamgee. Rather than checking the messages she called him.

The phone rang once before the doctor picked up. "Cassidy, how soon can you be ready to travel?" he said by way of hello. "Is tomorrow good?"

Still not used to the focused manner in which he always communicated, it took Cassidy a moment to reply. "Yes, late tomorrow should be fine, I should be able to clear up the end of semester work by then and be ready to go wherever you need."

"Good, I'll email the details to you shortly," was all he said before cutting the connection.

Once the details came through—a world which seemed temperate setting off the tech-alarms in a big way; portal just on the outskirts of town—she gathered together the small bag she usually travelled with and turned in for the night. The next morning, she went into the office and graded the remaining papers as quickly as she could.

One of the benefits of teaching a first-year class was that she could more or less scan the papers to see if they got the gist of the major concepts and only seldom had to dig deeper into the papers than her own knowledge. Occasionally, she would have to muddle through an awkward sentence and correct some small details, but she was pleasantly surprised to find that she had finished grading and was entering her final comments shortly after noon. With her teaching officially concluded for the year, scant pay and all, she made her way to the co-ordinates the doctor had sent her.

Two bus rides and a short hike later, she found herself on a hillside overlooking the main highway out of town. The straight line of the roadway extending to the south, towards the larger population centres, was nearly deserted at the now late hour. The co-ordinates she had been given said she was in the right place, but given the terrain and normal errors within GPS systems she knew she'd have a bit of a hunt ahead of her. She took the portal detection device which the professor had given her when she returned from her last outing and turned it on.

Making slow sweeping circles about, she listened for the pinging noise that would tell her which direction she needed to head. After a moment she realized it was indicating an up-hill trek. As the pinging grew more consistent, she quickened her pace over the icy ground, not caring that her feet slipped with every other step. An adventure waited and that was just what she needed right now, something to help her forget the current mess of her life on this planet. She had just entered a small cave shimmering with light from deep within, when the pinging became a constant drone. A smile plastering itself across her face, she made her way in and through into her next new world.

CHAPTER TWO

Cassidy stepped through the portal into the swirling snow. 'Not the temperate climate I was expecting,' she thought and gathered her field coat more tightly around her. She looked behind her and scratched a series of quick symbols into the stone next to the rapidly fading door. She knew it would be there, invisible, when she returned and would need the guide to return to her world.

She debated stepping back through the doorway to get some warmer gear, but decided that pressing on would be quicker. She'd warm up as she went and hopefully this would be an easy in and out job like Gamgee had predicted. She did pull a hat and gloves out of her bag and put them on. She scanned the horizon through the blowing snow and faintly made out the shapes of buildings in the near distance, and began to head that way, hoping that whatever she needed would be in one of those buildings.

The trek was more difficult than she had expected. Although much of the journey was over heavily packed snow on what must have been a well-built road, more was through freshly fallen or newly drifted snow that often sucked at her upper thighs if she paused at all. She could not reconcile the briefing Doctor Gamgee had given her to the arctic conditions around her. The initial scans had shown moderate temperatures, daily rains, everything you'd expect for a climate-controlled region. Who would voluntarily subject themselves to mountains of snow and sub-zero temperatures?

Out of the corner of her eye she thought she saw a dark shape moving against the shifting whiteness of falling snow. Pressing onward to the buildings ahead, she turned to look in that direction and saw only the snow swirling. Again, that shape at the edge of her vision drew her attention. This time she saw a vaguely human shape towering towards her in through the drifting snow. She quickened her pace, moving as fast as she dared over the snowpack.

With the buildings now coming into clear sight, she glanced over her shoulder to see the large shape gaining on her. Though it was still obscured by the falling snow, it glided its shaggy body over the snow, more like skating than walking. With the cold settling into her joints, Cassidy found another burst of speed, sprinting over the snowpack faster than she thought wise, toward the nearest of the buildings.

When it came fully into view, it looked like a shopping mall. She scrambled through the snow alongside the building, searching for a door that might open and frantically looking behind her as the shaggy giant came closer. Finally, after running the length of two sides of the building she came to a downward slope. Following it down to a bank of doors she tried them one after the other until she felt one swing towards her. Jumping through it, she pulled it tight behind her, scrabbling for something to bar the door to keep whatever had been following her outside.

"Um, child, are you quite alright?" a voice from inside the building asked with clear concern. "You're acting like one of the family's guards are chasing you."

Cassidy spun around to see a group of people, very tall people, gathered behind her. Each held something which could be used as a weapon, ranging from spear-like objects to shovels and one or two guns in evidence. Without exception, each had the shaggy furred appearance of her recent pursuer, though she could now see they were outer garments the group wore.

"I was being chased by something," she began and cut herself off with a shriek as the door thundered behind her. The creature which had been following her was now at the door, knocking excitedly.

"Grant me entry!" it said loudly. "There's some half-dressed fool out here we need to get into the warm."

Realizing he must have meant her, Cassidy released her grip on the door and stepped away with a nervous chuckle. "I thought you were a yeti or sasquatch or something," she said as the door opened and a man in furs stepped through.

"I do not know what a yetil or squamsuch are, but I know you must be near frozen," he spoke with a musical accent. "Come, we must get you warm."

The group herded her towards a fire in the centre of the room, somebody handing her a porcelain bowl of a thin soup. "You need to get some heat back into you. What in the thirteen names were you doing out dressed like that?" the first voice asked.

"I was expecting this to be clothing enough for where I planned to go," Cassidy said simply. "What has happened to the weather here?"

"You must have come a long way to not know that the weather towers are no longer functioning as we intended but are instead doing exactly what their masters want them to. The families decided some time ago that they would freeze those of us who could not or would not pay the exorbitant rates they demand to keep the machines running. Everybody they didn't need to keep the towers operational, that is. Now the towers are nothing more than havens for the families and those in their immediate employ. It's a terrible way to run things. How long ago did you set out, child?"

Cassidy considered what she had just heard. "You mean people are doing this to you on purpose?"

"Not just us," a voice spoke from somewhere in the crowd, "everybody has been forced to take refuge wherever they can, in shopping centres, old schools, all the old emergency shelters that had been set up before the weather control devices were brought online. At least it's gotten us all together so we can try to keep each other going."

She looked about the room: nearly forty people were gathered about a fire surrounded by hanging blankets and a mixture of faux and real furs, huddled for warmth within the small circle so constructed.

"We've formed our little groups against the cold and pooled all the available resources we could, but with the snow falling nearly constant and all our means of production frozen out, we've nearly hit the end of our ropes.

We've been plundering nearby homes and stores, plus hunting whatever we can find. Luckily the cold snap they created has driven a lot of animals into the more settled areas they'd normally avoid."

"Somebody did this to you on purpose?" Cassidy repeated. "I can't believe that with the power to maintain perfect growing conditions that anybody would force you into living in another ice age. It just seems too hard to believe."

"When the device was brought online first, it had been funded through a mixture of private contributors and public grants. People just wanted an end to the harsh winters and scorching summers, so they all paid the extra taxes, looking forward to the day when we could finally bring our climate into something manageable. We had nightly rains, and pleasant days, and plentiful crops which grew in their time. It was a perpetual golden summer. Then the governments lost their control and all rights reverted to the thirteen families who had been the primary private investors. They decided that if they were to keep everything running then the populace would have to pay for the privilege of having the weather guaranteed. At first those of us who could afford to pay did, but not everybody could afford to pay the rates they wanted, so the governments decided to start taxing people to make up the shortfalls. When people and the government weren't making the fees the families wanted, the governments tried to buy back their shares of the devices and enforce regulations that would force the families to maintain the climate within acceptable levels. In response, the families barred their towers, with only those workers they deemed vital to the maintenance of their way of life in the complexes. Loyal employees and necessary workers for the rowers to function were brought in to live out the self-imposed siege of cold the families brought down on us. That was somewhere around four cycles ago. Now all of us on the outside are running low on fuel and food, huddling in masses like this to stay warm but not letting our groups expand too much in fear of using up our stockpile too quickly. How do you not know this? Where have you been all this time that you didn't know all of this, child?"

Cassidy sipped her soup thoughtfully while considering her options on how to respond. "Would it make sense to you if I said I was outside the range of the towers? And that despite all appearances I'm not actually a child? Where I come from, I'm considered about average for a fully grown adult."

"Then you must not be from anywhere on this planet," the man replied.

"I'm not, I'm from an alternate dimension where we have no control over the weather but we can skip through dimensions," Cassidy said.

There was a brief moment of silence then everybody laughed. "Oh, child," a man said. "There will be no punishment here, we simply wish to send word to your shelter that you are safe." This statement was followed by nods all around.

Cassidy finished her soup and said, "I really am an adult, and not from this world. I've got credentials which should be ample proof of what I say," she added, reaching into her shoulder bag. "I know I'm shorter than you all are but trust me, fully grown adult."

"Then why do you speak our language so well," a voice from the crowd asked with skepticism. "You expect us to believe that you just randomly popped in from a different universe speaking our language?"

A murmur ran through those assembled as Cassidy responded, "To be honest, I'm having trouble with that one myself. I've run into language barriers in the past but I've also been in places where there isn't one. I just travel, looking for useful things to take home."

"Okay, we'll accept that you are who and what you say," the man from outside said. "But we're going to have to discuss what to do with you. You're free to roam within this shopping compound, but you can't go outside dressed like that. And nobody is leaving here until morning anyway. We'll find you somewhere to sleep and then figure out how best for us all to proceed tomorrow. Ursula, can you find some extra bedding for our 'off-worlder' please?"

"Sure," a young woman said. "Domina, please come with me. We'll try to find some better garb while we're about it." As Ursula ushered Cassidy away, the gathered crowd resumed discussions.

CHAPTER THREE

Ursula led Cassidy deeper into the building. "This was a shopping compound, before the government turned it into a weather shelter. At first, we respected the locked doors and used only what was given. Then we started using items in the found lost bins; eventually we decided to simply use whatever was in the building as a whole. The thirteen took everything they valued into their compounds and most of what was left would have expired anyway. As it is, we had to throw much of the food stuffs into the oubliettes," the woman explained.

Cassidy looked about what she thought of as a mall before she said, "In cases of disaster I think it's more than fair to use whatever resources are at hand. Besides the system here sounds much like the one at home: all the resources in the hands of a few with everybody else having to pay extortionate rates for a very small piece of the pie. Not even really a piece of the pie, just a sliver of the crust that we think is a piece."

Ursula looked at her, confused. "What is peye?"

Cassidy, unsure how to respond, simply stared back at the young woman. "You don't have pie here?"

Ursula looked uncertain how to respond.

"It's like fruit baked between crusts," Cassidy began. "You know what? It isn't important. The point is that there should be enough to go around, with everybody getting a portion that isn't just crap. Sorry, I'm not having the best day. I left a bit of mess behind at home, and I feel more than a little out of my element coming here to find something completely different than I was led to expect."

Ursula directed her into what at home Cassidy would have called a department store. "In here we can find bed clothing and appropriate garbing for you," she said. "What were you led to believe you'd find here? A perfect land of flutter-bys and sunshine, where the only work people did was to better their fellows, like in creche tales?" As she spoke, she guided Cassidy towards a rack of what looked like sleeping bags. "Surely none of these so-called dimensions you've seen has presented anything like that. People need to trade something they value to get other things they value, that's a basic drive among people-kind. That or they need to seize what they desire from others. To think otherwise shows a clear lack of understanding basic psychology. The only thing that prevents people from behaving so all the time is fear of repercussion. This bedding should be sufficient, we tend to cluster near the heat source at night to maintain our relative heat."

Cassidy was dumbstruck. To receive a lesson in the bleakest form of capitalism from a willowy young woman in an alternate dimension which so nearly reflected her own dismal thoughts from earlier in the week was beyond shocking. "I always hope for better. I want people to be better to each other," she responded in a subdued voice.

"I always believe that there is goodness at the core of all people. But I'm always disappointed, I guess. Something about me just doesn't want to admit the reality of it all: that greed is more commonplace than virtue. Let's find me a cool jacket like your people all wear, maybe some chocolate too."

Ursula only gestured to a different portion of the store in response. As the pair made their slow way through the store Cassidy noticed that many of the shelves and racks were empty. What remained were items that seemed to have little use in the frozen wastelands she had made her way through on her way to this shelter. Swimming suits, light outer wear that made her own gear seem more than adequate for the cold, and a variety of items which she didn't recognize. "Most of what's left here, you can't use it, now can you?" she asked.

"We could use much of it, if we wanted to expire from the conditions," Ursula replied. "Much of it simply has no use in the conditions the thirteen allow us to live in, and much of what we could use has been taken back to their towers for the use of the families and their selected. We make use of what is available and of value to us. The rest we allow to sit here until we can find some use for it. Unfortunately, that means much that was available is spoken for. Meanwhile, other items like that bathing garb has no practical application."

The pair continued on until they reached an outerwear section. "Much of what remains will have been too small for most of us, perhaps something will fit your slighter frame. If not, we will seek out the younglings' section to select from their larger pieces," Ursula said. "Perhaps it is a good thing you are slighter than the average Tellan."

Cassidy quickly chose a hooded black jacket in a material which reminded her of the serge favoured for military dress uniforms on Earth. Then she quickly donned a pair of charcoal coloured trousers over her own outfit. Tall brown boots and gloves of a matching animal hide completed the ensemble. She gave herself a quick lookover in a nearby mirror, which Ursula called a "self-viewer", and decided she looked not just stylishly ready for the cold but also like the type of professional who had often come to dig sites for photo ops and handshakes during public relations campaigns. Most importantly, she felt warm for the first time since she had stepped through the gate. "This should keep me warm enough and allow me to function," she said. "Will it pass muster among the local fashionistas?"

"It does look rather elegant and sufficiently warm, unless the thirteen decide to make conditions completely unlivable rather than simply unbearable," the slight Tellan replied. "What is a fash-on-ista?"

"Just me being silly," Cassidy giggled. "It isn't something that really matters, but aside from the height do I look enough like a local to blend in?"

Ursula stared at Cassidy blankly. "Do you mean will anybody assume you are not of this dimension?" When Cassidy nodded, Ursula replied, "Nobody will think you could be from another dimension so no matter what you wear it will be assumed you are from somewhere on Tellas."

The pair were interrupted by a commotion near the courtyard where everybody had been gathered.

CHAPTER FOUR

The two ran to the indoor courtyard to see portions of the glass-like ceiling crashing to the floor. The gathered crowd was already in action, some clearing the debris, while others hastily constructed supports to block the newly formed hole in the roof of their shelter.

"Just another fracture in the structure," a male voice called. "We'll have this sorted in short order. Will you two younglings lend a hand with the detritus while the usual crew places the patch on the canopy?"

"Earliest graduate in my seating, five years as a constructor of buildings, and all they let me do is tend stray younglings and empty oubliettes," Ursula muttered, ushering Cassidy toward the others cleaning the mess beneath the work area. "I have told them countless times that as the portions shatter it weakens the whole and we should simply reinforce the entirety of the canopy. Yes, it will darken the room considerably to do so with the materials we have on hand but it will allow us to retain the heat rather than allow it to escape and endanger more lives with each collapse."

Cassidy looked to her companion, "That seems a pretty specific complaint to have of your living mates. Can I ask why they treat you this way?"

"Because I am female and too old to be a youngling, but not old enough to be an adult in their minds," Ursula responded. "No woman younger than forty years can be considered competent in her field. No male younger than forty-five can either for that matter." The pair began to sweep away snow, watching the debris carefully for broken glass. The snow was collected in bins to melt, for use as wash water Ursula told her. That which might contain glass or other contaminants was taken outside and placed in the oubliettes. Once the mess was cleared, the small settlement gathered around the fire and began preparing for sleep.

The group placed a collection of sleeping mats in a circle around the fire. All the sleeping bags were placed within arm's reach of each other, maximizing the sharing of body heat. Cassidy marvelled at the space the group would share.

Ivan said, "We tried sleeping separately in the earlier times of the coldness, but found that even with fire-minders we would awaken in the night shivering. Many of us began to cluster without thought, preserving our heat by sharing it much as we do with our food. Now we bundle together when the night begins. Those who take the watch are given separate clusters to let the others sleep, but nobody is given watch for more than two nights running, and is never given duty the day after. We have even found light and sound protectors for those who have difficulty with being part of the evening huddles," he concluded, offering Cassidy a sleep mask and ear plugs.

She accepted the offered items with a hearty thank you but selected a place in the sleeping circle between Ursula and an elderly woman Cassidy guessed was an aunt; the woman had been introduced as mother-sister. Excepting the six designated watchers, and four fire-watch, the company settled in to sleep. Perhaps fifty people, huddled together in a circle around a fire burning in the central concourse of a shopping centre in an entirely different dimension than her own, Cassidy Cane felt more relaxed and at home than she had since she shared an apartment with multiple roommates during her undergraduate programme. She was lulled into a peaceful slumber by the breathing of the other sleepers, the pacing of the sentries, and the regular actions of the fire-minders.

The next morning, she awoke chilled and stiff, but well rested despite that, and was fed from the dwindling supplies available to the small group of survivors. Ivan and Ursula were arguing quietly in a corner of the atrium when Cassidy approached them.

"Will you please tell this addle-headed male that we need to reinforce the roof before more damage is done by snow accumulation," Ursula snapped.

"And will you please tell my daughter that more mature people than her have had their say in the matter and we shouldn't involve a stranger, especially not a stranger who claims to be from another dimension," Ivan snapped vehemently.

Cassidy held up her hands. "Leave me out of any arguments, but let me into a debate," she said. "The ceiling will continue to break if more snow falls. It happens on Earth every winter, that's part of why I came here to get the plans for the weather control device. As for my claims of being from a different dimension; I've shown you my identification, what more do you want?"

"You've seen a natural progression of weather cycles?" Ivan asked, disbelief clear in his voice. "Since the weather control devices were set to working nobody has seen that and it is not possible that you are old enough for that."

Cassidy fumbled through her bag to show him the identification she had mentioned. "If you look at this, you'll see the proof of at least some of what I say: it shows that I'm in my twenties and that—" She cut herself off as her cellphone hit the floor. She picked it up, quickly checked the screen for cracks and tested that it still worked, then slid it back into her bag.

The pair looked at her in shock. "You've never seen a smartphone before? You can build these amazing buildings and contraptions to control your planet but you don't have phones?" she asked incredulously.

"We have computers, but nothing that small," Ivan replied. "Every home has a wing set aside for the controlling computer, and they can't do what you just did with that tiny thing. How have you miniaturized the vacuum tubes to such an extent? How does the screen-only interface function?"

"And how do you make the images so clear? The text so clear I could read it some of it from here?" Ursula asked.

It was now Cassidy's turn to be shocked. "You still use vacuum tube transistors here? We haven't used those for any practical applications in decades. I don't know when they were abandoned for computing purposes but these days, they're only used for entertainment purposes. Everything is done on microchips with integrated circuits. I don't know all the science behind it, that wasn't my field of study, but this uses a more durable solid-state type of chip." She trailed off at the confused looks on their faces. "These are common in my dimension, common enough that most people always have one on them, even when they know they're going somewhere that they'll lose the network they function on. I carry this the same way I carry a pen or a pocket knife, it's just something I have when I leave the house."

"Truly you are not from this world," Ivan responded. "Though you are still barely bigger than a child."

"I told you she doesn't behave like children do, father," Ursula said. "Listen to the wisdom she speaks, even if you refuse to listen to it from me. We need to take steps to keep the roof overhead, then perhaps we should assist her in her mission."

Ivan looked from Cassidy to Ursula, and then to the ceiling. After a long silence he said, "Very well, I shall designate a team to work with you to make our people safe. I will take a small hunting party and guide Cassidy to the archives. There we might find that which she seeks."

About half an hour later, by the watch on Cassidy's wrist, Ursula had a small crew of workers collecting materials. Ivan had a team of three outfitted in heavy duty outdoor gear, each armed with a rifle and something which looked like a cross between a sling and a bow, similar to an atlatl but larger in scale than she was used to seeing. 'An unsurprising development given the stature of the locals,' Cassidy thought. 'I guess it would be similar to the sizing of clothes and scaling of other implements; you make it to fit the user.'

Cassidy, Ivan, and their team donned snow shoes, and left their shelter shortly after the work began on the shelter.

CHAPTER FIVE

"The snow should be less vigorous today," Ivan said. "The families have stopped short of trying to murder all of us who live outside the towers. They seem intent to simply torture us with the cold and precipitation. The public archives are little more than a furlong along the roadway so we should reach it in short order, the hunters were all law enforcement in the past and will both protect us as we travel and seek food for our return."

Cassidy simply nodded and followed the group in the direction indicated. Feeling more protected in the group than she had while fleeing the unknown the day before, she took better notice of her surroundings. The buildings, what was visible beneath the snow at least, were similar in many aspects to those on Earth, but were of a different scale entirely. Clearly built to accommodate the natives of this world. They were constructed of wood, stone, or some material which she did not recognize. 'A local stone, or concrete-like material,' she filed the thought away for later consideration.

The streets ran in straight lines, meeting at nearly perfect right angles. She wondered if they aligned to any strict directional markers, as the North to South or East to West tendency in some cities on Earth. Instead of questioning this, she focused on the names on the buildings and the turnings they took in case she was separated from her guides and needed to find her way back to their base. Ivan led them in a straight line, without deviation from their desired destination, the others of the group seemed to split their attentions to search the streets they did not take.

"What are they watching for?" Cassidy asked, indicating their companions.

Ivan looked back. "They watch for predators and prey. They will defend us if they must. Or feed my people if they can. We have learned that if we must journey then we should collect what food we can. While we explore the archives for what you seek, they will search for sustenance, textbooks for the younglings, and anything else that was requested before we left. They have lists of things missed by those who dwell within our shelter."

"You've been sequestered long enough that you have a dedicated scouting party?" Cassidy asked in surprise.

"They were all employed to deliver different things before the snows came. Sulva delivered packages from city to city. Flavius brought foods from restaurants to private dwellings. Claud delivered and installed computers. They are familiar with the layout of the community and were often called upon to defend themselves against the creatures who lurk within and without the community."

"I'm headed to the library with delivery drivers as an honour guard," Cassidy muttered. "It's like a tale from the wild west and some goof in a white hat will appear around the next corner to save the day."

Ivan chuckled softly. "I admit it does sound like a work of cheap fiction designed to entertain, at least that's how I interpret your words. This is the world we live in; people do their best in the circumstance."

A low growl from the crossing street ahead silenced them. Two of the guards, Cassidy thought it was the ones named Claud and Sulva, edged forward, each facing opposing directions along the cross street. Atlatl raised, Flavius walked behind them, scanning the upper floors of the buildings around them. A large creature resembling a koala in shape but coloured like a panda lumbered into view and all three hunters backed away.

"Keep back," Sulva called. "They usually wander off when they see people. So, we'll give this one the chance to survive."

Cassidy watched the creature waddle ponderously to a nearby building, then marvelled as it gracefully scaled the ornate work on the façade of the building. "Are they dangerous?" she asked in a hushed voice.

"Not at all, there were few cineleucia left before the weather was altered and we seek to protect those that remain," Ivan responded, then added with a small grin, "Besides, I hear they taste horrible."

The cineleucia had stopped on a ledge of the building it was climbing and seemed to be settling down for a nap when Sulva waved them on. Cassidy was sure she could hear the creature snoring as they passed. "They mostly sleep wherever they can, move to find food, and then sleep again. Most of them escaped from the custody we had them in, others like them were drawn by the calls of those who had freed themselves," Sulva said in quiet tones, her eyes searching their surroundings the whole time

"Custody?" Cassidy asked.

"Yes, we had some in protective enclosures, along with other animals. Younglings would take learning trips to see the creatures being cared for in such parks, we called them menageries. Many of the creatures who wander the city now were released or escaped their custody in menageries. Those we know are plentiful and edible we eat. The ones who cannot survive in such conditions as we have now are mercied. The others we let make their own survival," the delivery driver shook her head sadly. "It is not the ideal situation, for them or us, but life must be preserved."

The rest of the journey was passed in silence and with no larger incident than the occasional slide on the slippery road surface.

The Archives turned out to be a large, plain building made of the same concrete-like material as many of the other buildings. 'They may be great engineers here but their art and expression leave a lot to be desired, at least down among the groundlings,' Cassidy thought. 'I guess that doesn't vary much with the basically human species, no matter what particular dimension they happen to live in.'

The window opened easily for them and the five entered what might well have been the largest indoor space Cassidy had ever seen. Ivan pointed in what looked like a random direction, "Most of the technological works will be in that portion of the archives on the third floor. I will guide Cassidy there and assist her search. The rest of you should seek the requested items, retrieve any medic supplies and food you discover unless challenged. The Archives have been unvisited since the trouble began, but some determined soul may have decided to change their residence since our last visit. We will meet back here in one klukkutima. We dare risk no longer for fear of a change in the atmospheric conditions." The group all agreed and quickly set about their errands.

The building was silent save for the passage of the small group, their footfalls quietly echoing before being swallowed by the neatly shelved and stacked books. Ivan pulled a small electric light from his pocket and turned it on, casting a small circle of light about himself and Cassidy. They made their way to the side of the building and entered a stairway. As they climbed, he spoke, "These are places of study, material is borrowed as needed and returned afterwards. Speech here is discouraged so as not to interfere with the work of others. Even if it appears that we are the only ones present I prefer to maintain that rule."

Cassidy simply nodded her agreement as they exited the stairway. She followed Ivan to what she would have called a card catalogue in a library on Earth only to discover that it was exactly that. The filing system seemed to be different, using symbols rather than numbers, and the writing seemed to be a mixture of scripts closely resembling Cyrillic and Greek alphabets but not being strictly either. "I can't read your language," she whispered to her guide.

"These are just the symbols employed in libraries to

indicate where certain topics might be found," he answered. "Perhaps you will understand our written words as well as you do our speech." Cassidy was hopeful but unconvinced. After all she didn't need to be able to read the plans herself, as long as she found the right ones.

Ivan made a quick note on a small slip of something that looked like paper and gestured for her to follow. Part of Cassidy felt like a fugitive, hiding from some crazed pursuer. Another part of her felt the calm inherent in all libraries. The mass of the books quieting the footsteps of all who passed among the ordered rank and file of shelves and bookcases, the mingled scents trapped within the pages from those who had used the books previously, the predictable layout of the shelves, and the knowing that almost anything you could desire to know could be found on hand, provided that somebody had researched and written on the topic. Libraries were a comfort to almost every academic and nerdy kid she knew, and she was more at home than she had been anywhere in a very long time.

At random she drew out a book and flipped through it. The writing employed an alphabet much like Latin but different enough that she could only read one word in ten. A quick glance at the illustrations led her to believe the volume to be a user manual for some sort of food preserver, one meant to dehydrate massive amounts of grain. The next book she took down appeared to describe the machinery employed to make pickles in an industrial setting. "Are all the books in this library dedicated to industrial food preparation?" she inquired.

"No, just those in this specific section. The third floor

is dedicated to all industry, we just happen to be in the nutrition preparation section," the burly guide responded. "Do you not have similar repositories on your world? How would you separate them?"

Embarrassed slightly, Cassidy responded, "We do, in many cases we dedicate those repositories to specific topics. We call them libraries or archives too, though. I was just surprised to see these many manuals together."

"Just ahead we should find information on the machines used for travel; after that the weather towers, if I am remembering correctly. Most of my time here was spent on the other floors, pursuing other topics," Ivan said. "The information guide pointed us this way at any rate."

"I am sorry, it's been a long day. I was hoping I'd be able to walk in, find what I wanted, and return easily. I didn't expect all of," she gestured to the half-lit building and the view through the windows. "Well, just this; I didn't expect this. I expected warm days with optimal growing conditions and..."

"You describe a perfect world where all things are available for free to those who need them. Drink is available in streams and food grows on trees and nobody charges for them?" Ivan asked.

"Yeah, big rock candy mountain," she muttered.

"We have a song about the place you speak of, a fairy tale told to lazy children," he replied.

"We have it in my world too," she said. "We also have an expression that claims that nothing is free."

"Such is the dream of many, though there will always be one to tell you that what you pay for is better than what is given," Ivan commented thoughtfully. "Surely the survival of the individual and the desire to better one's state can coexist without causing harm to one another. Ah, now is not the time for such thoughts, let us see if the volumes you desire are here and we can pursue such thought exercises as we fill our bellies around a warm fire."

Cassidy nodded, waiting for her guide to indicate when they reached the shelf they sought. The quiet of the archive, relaxing at first, now left more room in her head for her anxieties to echo. She wondered if she would be forced to live in the library when she went back to Earth, like the urban legend she had heard from students at nearly every university she had visited. She was relieved when Ivan said, "This unit."

CHAPTER SIX

The pair checked the shelves. "The records indicate that the documents you desire should be here," Ivan said as he scanned the spines of the volumes shelved there. "In this empty slot."

"Maybe they were just shelved wrong," Cassidy said and began browsing the shelves at random, hoping she would recognize what she was looking for if she saw it.

After individually checking each volume on the shelf Cassidy asked, "Is there a sorting area, where the plans might have been laid after somebody had them out for study?"

Ivan nodded and guided her to a rolling cart full of books awaiting their return to the shelves. As he inspected the few titles on the cart he said, "There are two of these for each floor."

"One for the floor it's on and one for other floors," Cassidy replied, some things being universal to libraries and archives no matter what dimension they were in. "Will we have time to check them all?"

"If we hurry, we may," the stoic man replied. "The others will await our return regardless."

The pair made their way swiftly through the building, finding no sign of the desired documents. When Cassidy and Ivan met the others at the main entrance, they were greeted with a collection of what looked to Cassidy like first aid kits, snack foods, and books. Sulva and Claud were separating the items into convenient carry packages while Flavius kept watch.

"The weather seems to be worsening," Flavius said. "I hope everybody has found what they sought because we'll have to make our way back to the shelter swiftly."

Cassidy swiftly explained what she was looking for and what had happened as the goods were divided amongst the quintet. Claud said, "The families ordered those documents pulled from all public archives before the troubles began. Had I known that was what we were looking for I could have saved us this trip."

Flavius looked to their packs, "We have plenty to show for the trip at any rate, so it was not wasted. Let's get back before travelling becomes harder. I never thought I'd say that about travel within a community before all this started."

They started back towards the shelter, Cassidy and Ivan walking sullenly while the others chatted about the items they had found and marvelling that nobody had more thoroughly explored the archives before. The winds were gusting higher than before, kicking dervishes of snow into the air and making the passage more difficult.

"We'll stay closer to the buildings on this side of the roadway," Sulva shouted to the group as the wind tried to snatch her breath away. "We'll take the extra shelter from the wind where we can, besides everything should be bedded down out of the storm at this time of day."

The group trudged forward. Cassidy, while thankful for the fact that it would be a straight line to their destination, trusted the Tellans to ensure they didn't miss their destination. 'Why did I think this would be such an easy mission for a change? Just stroll into a library and check out a book, easier than falling off a bike.' Her thoughts were rudely interrupted by the roars of the cineleucia. The creature stood before them, forepaws raised, claws extended.

Sulva, who had been leading the expedition party, raised both hands and started backing away from the five-meter-tall bear-like specimen. She waved for the team to circle around the bear, swinging wide into the street. The bear roared its defiance as they started around, going silent when the group stopped and began to back away again. Sulva decided to try again, this time leading the group to the other side of the roadway before attempting to resume their forward progress. The cineleucia renewed its roaring, this time lumbering a few steps toward them and slashing the air with its razor-sharp forepaws.

The terrified group stopped. Sulva shouted something but the wind carried her voice away unheard. Instead she gestured again, and ran for the door of the closest building. Using the carrysac full of books, she smashed a window and waved to the others as they sprinted inside. Then she closed the door firmly behind her, or tried to at least around the now trapped forepaw of the cineleucia. Cassidy, having seen similar situations, grabbed Sulva in a bear hug, first leaning to open the door, then throwing her weight fully backwards. On her third try Sulva joined her in repeating the motion, repeatedly slamming the door on the cineleucia's paw until the beast withdrew its paw and fled with a roar that rattled the door.

As the two caught their breath Flavius looked out through the nearest windows. "I don't think it's gone far. What could cause a cineleucia to behave in such a manner?"

Claud shrugged. "A bunch of things, like a mate or offspring. Both of which would be great news it would just mean avoiding this stretch of the roadway for however long the bear decides to call this patch its home. Guess we need to find another way back home though. Any ideas?"

Ivan looked around the building, "Maybe there is another entrance we can use on next parkway, and then we might return to the roadway we were using?" Cassidy and Sulva, still slightly winded from their encounter with the cineleucia, waved the group into motion, following them deeper into the building.

CHAPTER SEVEN

The group made their way deeper into the building, past open-faced lockers and a trophy case. "Was this a school?" Cassidy asked. "A place for the education of younglings, I mean."

Ivan nodded in response. "It was where they learned the basic skills they would require for chosen career paths, preparatory to higher education."

"Younglings study here to their eighteenth year and then either enter the working forces or pursue more education," Claud clarified. "We would do well to search for further supplies as we search for a way out."

"We stay together and make our way swiftly on," Ivan said. "The day is short and we must return to the shelter before dark, lest we worry the others."

The others readily agreed, making their way deeper into the school as silently as possible, their footsteps echoing in the abandoned hallways and empty classrooms. The dim sunlight through the windows creating eerie shadows all about the small, slow moving group, they ventured onward. Claud and Sulva checked each classroom they passed, sometimes finding small first aid kits or snacks in the desks, occasionally a hat or pairs of gloves, but mostly finding nothing more than dust and abandonment.

They had made it to the end of the corridor when they heard laughter behind them. They froze, looking about them in the dimly lit corridor. "Is somebody else in here?" Cassidy asked. Sulva repeated the question, in a louder voice so that it carried down the corridor. After a span of several heartbeats Cassidy thought she heard the sound of feet running in the distant darkness, and more giggling. "Is there somebody here?" she repeated, louder than Sulva. Again, nothing answered but the sound of scuttling feet and muffled giggles.

"It is crocuta," Ivan whispered in a trembling voice. "If they are the larger ones we must flee, if the smaller ones we will be fine."

"Crocuta?" Cassidy asked.

Flavius answered, "Pray we don't see them; terrifying creatures that will eat anything they can sink their teeth into. We often find them in the unused buildings. Like Ivan said, if it is the more common smaller ones, we'll be fine. Either way there should be an exit up ahead. Keep moving."

The group seemed to move a little faster now, Cassidy needing to speed her steps to keep pace with the longer-limbed Tellans. She hadn't realized that they had been slowing themselves for her sake before she had started to fall behind. As they proceeded, the sounds of giggles and scuttling feet grew louder and closer. In panic, she glanced over her shoulder to see several pairs of glowing red eyes.

The sight leant her feet extra speed and she began

to gain ground on the others, soon passing Claud, who had been in the rear position. He sped as she passed him, matching her speed. The giggling grew louder and Cassidy again risked a glance over her shoulder, this time seeing mottled brown and black fur on squashed snouts below the still glowing eyes. One of the creatures let out a call that reminded her of the calls of the infamous laughing hyenas from Earth, but these creatures were little larger than, and strongly resembled, the dock rats she had seen in various seaports.

Some instinctive part of her still recoiled from the creatures, adding an extra shot of adrenaline into her system and extra speed to her step. "There had better be a door at the end of this hallway, or a window," she gasped as the crocuta began lunging around her feet. They didn't attack, playfully running ahead, then circling back to charge her again. She almost laughed at the capering creatures, while also inwardly shrieking in panic at them.

Over the laughter-punctuated pitter-patter of the rodent-like feet she heard the sound of a heavy window sliding open on rusty hinges and looked ahead to see a rectangle of light splitting the darkness before her. From somewhere deep down she found another burst of speed that carried her through the now open window and into the rapidly worsening storm, slamming the window closed behind them as the crocuta hit, first as a few falling pebbles, then as an avalanche.

Sulva edged toward the roadway they had been travelling when they entered the school and took a peek around the corner. Pleased with what she saw, the former delivery driver gestured urgently for the team to continue on their way. They filed out of the alleyway, each of them casting nervous glances either towards the window holding back the crocuta or cineleucia standing sentinel on their backtrail.

CHAPTER EIGHT

They returned to the shopping plaza at the height of the storm winds, battling the doors open between hurricane force gusts that whipped the snow in lashing strands that stung the face and blinded the eyes. Once inside they sat, backs to the door, panting for breath, rubbing hands and arms to return circulation to their extremities.

Ursula ushered them closer to the fire, under the newly reinforced ceiling, and gave them a hot beverage to drink that reminded Cassidy of heavily sweetened Darjeeling tea. Claud took the packs from the others and distributed the items they had retrieved from the archives. Flavius and Sulva reported on the new wildlife situation in equal parts hope, at the potential mating of a pair of cineleucia, and despair, at the detour it would mean for travel in the area.

Cassidy sat glumly before the fire as the snow melted on her clothing, the damp fabric adding to her overall feeling of misery. She ate what she was offered without tasting it, though the sensation of having a full belly brought up her mood somewhat. When Ursula came to take the empty bowl away Cassidy asked, "If the plans were taken from the archives where would they be now?"

"They'd need to keep copies in the towers," Ursula responded. "I assume you mean the plans for the weather towers themselves; they would need to have a copy for maintenance at the towers. That is an issue for tomorrow. The issue for right now is getting you into something dry and properly warmed up to face the night. Come, I have some dry clothing that should fit well enough." Cassidy took the clothing, changed, and hung her wet items to dry. She sat and watched the fire silently until she drifted off to sleep.

In the morning she approached Ursula, "Where is the nearest tower?"

Ursula gave Cassidy a confused look.

"Any tower will do," Cassidy continued. "I just need to know where it is, get a really good look at it, and I can figure out the rest for myself; but some idea of how to begin would be a big help."

"Cassidy, I don't think you've thought this out, you can't just," Ursula began but Cassidy interrupted.

"Of course, I haven't thought it out, that's why I'm asking you questions about the tower. I need to know everything I can about the tower before I make a full plan," the archaeologist said. "I need to research the place, and figure out how best to get in and.... I don't know what else but I know I need to get those plans and make my way home to deal with the mess I currently call my life."

Ursula took a moment to examine the feisty and, to her, diminutive figure. "First, we'll eat, then we will seek out books from the bookseller here in the plaza and make decisions from there. I know there are people here who have been in the nearest tower; we can talk to them as well, after we have eaten. Please, Cassidy, I'll help but right now I'm hungry."

The pair made their way to the line for food and each took a bowl of thin gruel. Cassidy, being too excited to eat, passed her bowl to Ursula, who ate both bowls of the gruel with great satisfaction. Then the pair made their way to a book store within the plaza. The fiction and home maintenance sections were nearly empty, Ursula saying that their contents were probably with the residents near the main shelter area or taken to homes before the group had taken refuge in the shelter. The rest of the shop, including the science, technology, and tourism sections were largely intact. The pair scoured the volumes they could find about the towers, especially those focused on the local tower.

"It turns out that the Steward Tower had a museum before the expulsion," Ursula said. "It may be the easiest way to sneak into the building, although this says that it had no direct access to the rest of the tower."

"Maybe not the best way in then," Cassidy responded. "This book has a map that shows multiple entries on each side of the building, but I still haven't figured out the writing here and can't read how it's labelled."

"Secure entrance, private entrance, office entrance," Ursula responded, pointing to a different set of markings each time. "I know that before the lockouts those entrances required keys or were guarded; I would think that now all would be more heavily guarded than before, if not simply closed forever."

The pair turned back to their books, periodically choosing new ones on the same topic. Eventually they had built towers out of the books about the Steward Tower. Feeling like she had absorbed all the knowledge on the topic which she could from the books in the store, and having gone through all the books about the Steward Tower she could find, Cassidy stood and stretched her back.

"Now let's see if we can find some food and primary sources on the topic," she said. At a questioning look from Ursula she clarified, "Now we look for people who have been in the building, anybody who had family living in the tower or who worked there or might have visited the building; and learn whatever we can from them. But first we need food, scholarship is hungry work."

The two returned to the fire once more, queueing for whatever food might be available. Once again, the thin gruel, this time bolstered with some dried bread that had been retrieved from either the school or the archives. "Have supplies grown so low already?" Ursula asked the man portioning out of the food.

"The parties were sent out yesterday; some haven't returned, some returned with empty carrysacs," he answered. "What was brought back is being distributed as we process it, but I was ordered to tighten rations while a full accounting is done. Truthfully, I feel supplies are not that low yet, but will be soon."

The pair walked a short distance off, Ursula savouring each bite as if it might be her last. Cassidy, eating slowly and thoughtfully, said, "I guess this means that any plan to infiltrate the tower should involve a plan to set the weather to rights as well. Not much point in letting this go on much longer if we'll potentially be in a position to solve both our problems at once."

Ursula finished her small meal and stared into the fire glumly. "This could require more research and planning than we initially anticipated," she said morosely. "I will return to the bookseller to see if I can discover anything else. You should begin your queries to see who may have knowledge of the Steward Tower."

With their easy agreement, Ursula set off into the shopping plaza. Cassidy began doing interviews with those who remained in the shelter that day, only now seeking those who had worked with the machinery as well as those who had simply been to the tower. At first many of those in residence were eager to talk; though Cassidy's notebook made many uneasy, they were simply glad to converse with the new person after so long cooped up with the same people; but it soon grew apparent that few of those here had any useful knowledge on either the tower or the weather device. Gradually Cassidy came to realize that those who did have any practical knowledge of the tower were most likely those who had gone out with the gathering teams.

She put away her notebook and began instead to make herself useful about the shelter: tidying things, playing with the few younglings she hadn't realized were in residence, teaching them how to build slingshots from what was on hand, and just casually chatting about what she had seen during her trip outside on her previous journeys. Though she could offer little in the way of information to those she spoke with, the news of snow accumulations and general state of the buildings she had seen and entered was welcomed by those she spoke to.

She especially enjoyed making skipping ropes from

electrical cords for the younglings and teaching them some of the rhymes she remembered from her youth. Their smiles and laughter spread to all those who remained inside on the cold and blustery day; some of the less staid adults joined in with varying levels of success. It might not have been her most productive day, but Cassidy still felt it was a day well spent and was smiling herself when she went to her small bedroll before the search parties had returned from their expeditions.

CHAPTER NINE

The next morning, she awoke early, crept from her sleeping place quietly, and joined those awake by the fire to sip the always ready strong tea that many of the adults seemed to survive on. Discussion with the small group revealed that while there were sufficient supplies for a few months—provided the protein stores could be supplemented with game animals—it had been decided that everybody would begin rationing now rather than waiting until circumstances made the need truly dire.

"A few months to adjust to being hungry rather than a few days of having nothing," one of the fire-minders said. "We have enough firewood to keep us warm for much longer if we use all the furniture in this building but we need to send our gatherers farther afield to find more food and medicines."

"That seems a little pre-emptive to me, but it does make sense. I hope to make a few expeditions to see the tower in the next few days; hopefully I can assist the gathering teams rather than hinder them," Cassidy said.

"Ursula told me of your desire to speak with those who had been in the tower; a visual inspection was the next step I suspected you would take," Ivan said from behind her. Cassidy turned to see the man holding a tea cup. "I was one of the early fabricators of the weather control device. Design and manufacture, but never an operator. I did assist in the installation process and could possibly serve as a guide once you were inside the tower itself."

Cassidy stared at the man blankly for a moment. "You were on the design team?" she finally spluttered.

"Yes, I assisted in the design," Ivan said calmly. "I was one of fourteen engineers who created the rain distribution component of the device. There were approximately fifty other major components required to take full control of the climate, but the rain distributors were among the earliest developed, to guide precipitation into deserts and away from settlements and regions prone to flood."

"That makes perfect sense really, creating arable lands and reducing flood damage is a priority for my own people," Cassidy responded. "Once I figure out how to get inside you can take me where I need to go? That makes that much of the plan much easier."

Ivan smiled "I will tell the gatherers of the information you seek and we shall plot the proper course of action from there. Now I have responsibilities today, it is my duty to take a turn as gatherer today. Perhaps you can join me? I do intend to journey in that direction."

Cassidy chugged what remained of her tea. "Let me grab my gear and I can meet you by the door."

Moments later the pair met by the entryway to the shopping plaza. Ivan, once again dressed in the clothing he had worn to the archives; Cassidy decked out in a combination of her gear from Earth and her new clothing from Tellan stores. When asked if she had anything to hunt with, she produced a slingshot from the pocket of her Earth-side jacket.

"What is that?" Ursula, who had come to see them off, asked.

"It's called a slingshot," Cassidy said, then gave a brief explanation and demonstration of how to use the simple device. "They're easy to make and transport but best part is that almost anything small can be turned into ammunition for it. It does take some practice to use effectively, but I've been practising a lot lately."

Ivan remained dubious but agreed that it should serve the purpose for their expedition that day. Once outside in the clear morning, he turned them in the direction that Cassidy had come to think of as south for the planet. Her reckoning was based on the layout of the roads and streets in the community, based on the shelter in the shopping plaza being the centre of a Cartesian plane. The portal to Earth was sort of to the west, the archives were east, and that was all her travels had revealed.

"Our main purpose will be to check buildings for anything which might be of use to the people at our shelter," Ivan said. "Many of the closer structures have been harvested already so we will advance appropriately before we begin to search in earnest. We must also watch for edible fauna as we proceed: there may not be much on this course of travel as the confines where animals were held in captivity were nearer the archives and little of the wildlife has dared enter the community this deeply yet."

It was perhaps the longest speech Cassidy had heard the man make and she listened to every word as she looked more closely at the architecture in this portion of the small city. It was much like what she had seen elsewhere, all straight lines and utilitarian dwellings built on a scale for those who lived there, nothing stood out save the numbered roadways they passed. She had grown familiar enough with the script used here to recognize that they had just crossed the intersection of fifteenth roadway and twentieth street. After a short march in silence they crossed twenty-first street and Cassidy could picture the neatly gridded lines she had seen on one of the maps in the bookseller the day before. Seward Tower was on the corner of twentieth and one-hundred-ninety-third, perhaps two days travel from their shelter, based on their current rate of travel.

Ivan had resumed talking while Cassidy had been doing these calculations and something he said caught her attention. "Did you say that we'd return to the shelter tomorrow?"

"That is the plan, yes," he spoke in the same calm tones he seemed to always use. "I have bedding for our use, we will use any empty building we can find. Some of the buildings still have the original residents, or some who moved in after the troubles began, but most are in the emergency shelters established after the families began to punish those outside the towers. Our shelter is the nearest to the Steward's home, so shelter will be easy to find; we may even use one of those established by previous expeditions. Perhaps I should have told you this before we left but I had not thought it important: all our gathering expeditions are two-day affairs now that we have to venture further with each trip."

"No, not a problem at all. I just," Cassidy began. "Okay, yeah maybe I'm a little surprised but I can deal. It'll give me a chance to examine your world as it is. Is all the community built like this, the straight lines and lack of ornamentation?" she asked, hoping to distract herself with stories from her guide and hunting companion.

"Most of Aetalus was built to provide support for the weather tower. The towers had to be built within a specific range to ensure that the entire planet could receive the effects. There was nothing here before the plans for the climate controller were finalized. When work began on the precipitation redirectors there was nothing here beyond a road linking other communities. It was, to quote my daughter, untamed wilderness," Ivan replied. "I believe that is the sole reason we receive as much wild game as we do. The land was improperly cleared and the animals desire to return to their habitat rather than establish new ones."

Cassidy nodded reflexively, then processed what she had heard. "You're saying this is a new city and that it's a company town to boot?" she asked.

Ivan took a moment before responding "If you mean of recent construction only for the commercial purpose of the weather tower, then yes. There are many portions of this community that you would find similar to other communities, but that was a designed aspect of the new community. Some developments were made to make this community a model for others, such as the grid of the streets instead of a random assortment of straight lines and curves."

"It must make learning the navigation of the community easier," Cassidy commented.

"Yes, but it removes some of the art from the streets. The normal vitality of a community can be seen in the curve of the roads, the natural grouping of like-minded people. Here there is an arts centre on one side of the community, an actor's pavilion near the centre, and schools of rhythmic movement in a different portion of the community entirely. None of them near each other," Ivan spoke reproachfully. "It was a plan that put little thought into being an actual community, but yes, numbered roadways and streets that proceed in an orderly manner is good."

They walked for a moment in silence before Cassidy spoke again. "I guess there were some faults in their logic. Like most towns built to support an industry where I come from; the basics like work and accommodation are pretty well thought out. Everything else, all the things that go into living a life outside of work, gets shoved in wherever it'll fit. A cinema here, shopping centre over there, green space on the edge of town."

Ivan looked to her thoughtfully. "Yes, I feel it should all be balanced, like a circuit: the power source is industry; the workers are the current; all other aspects of life are the resistors, capacitors, and transistor which allow the current to perform efficiently and perform the designated function. This machine lacked diodes to ensure the proper flow of power, the towers became the only inputs and outputs with all other current being forgotten by the design, this will cause a short circuit somewhere."

Cassidy quickly pored through her limited knowledge of technology. "You're saying that because they've neglected the excess charge they let into the system, something is going to malfunction?"

"Something has to," the former engineer said gravely. "Pressure in a water line causes leaks. Excess charge causes a short circuit. High friction will make two sticks catch fire. These are basic principals of physics. The signs of un-happiness were in the people before the families seized the weather makers, in more urban centres at least. Rural life had taken on idyllic terms of routine, balancing itself. There was never balance to be found here, just work, rest, and repeat; no space for enjoyment. I think the families may have brought the cold precipitates to distract us from these problems as much as to punish us for not paying what they desired. Fearing that the people would topple the rulers as they have in past times." He gestured for her to enter a building that looked no different than any other on their left. Cassidy thought it might be an apartment.

"Well, revolutions do have a way of coming around," Cassidy said as they stepped into a building not much warmer than the outside.

Ivan smiled broadly at her, "That they do. That they do."

CHAPTER TEN

The pair took a moment to look around the corridor of the building they had entered. A hallway, lined with doors, ended with a stairwell reaching into the higher floors. Ivan briefly consulted a series of markings on the wall before saying, "This building has been checked. The third room on this side has a warming station and temporary camp we can use if we wish to. I would like the opportunity to warm for a few moments if we can spare them."

Cassidy nodded and gestured for him to lead the way. She stepped into the room to see the walls had been hung with draperies, the floor had been lined with extra carpets, and a number of lanterns lay about the room with matches nearby. Once the door was closed and a lantern lit, the room began to warm. Cassidy hadn't realized how cold she had grown until the heat began to seep through her clothing.

Ivan, having doffed his hat and gloves, settled on a cushioned chair near the lantern he had lit. "I will show you each of these as we pass. Some will be like this, others more or less elaborate, but you should know how to find those between the shelter and the tower."

She nodded as he passed her a scrap of paper with symbols drawn in a precise hand. "These are the buildings where you will find the easiest shelters. I know you have trouble with our script but I know you can match symbols. Once inside each building you may have to hunt for the warming station but at least you will be inside."

"Thank you, but we won't be separated," Cassidy said. "I won't let you leave me behind or do that to you, at least not on this trip. Hopefully I won't be out alone before I return to my own world." She sat in a chair next to her guide and held her hands near the lantern. "This would not be a terrible place to spend an evening, if there were books here I could read."

He nodded silently, mimicking her hand gesture. "We should not dally over long here. We do have to check other dwellings on our way to the tower and it is not a short distance." Waiting for her to signal her readiness he extinguished the lantern and followed her back to the street.

Ivan stood silently, waiting for Cassidy to select the direction of travel. She led them up streets and roadways with only minor course corrections from the elder man. Occasionally he diverted them to a building, either to show her a shelter or to search for supplies; anything they found would be left for later collection, in a shelter or simply just within the entryway of the building they had found them in. The engineer kept careful notes of where things were, making similar notations on Cassidy's map as they progressed. The wind was beginning to rise when Cassidy first spotted the tower.

It rose above the neighbouring buildings like a tree in

a mossy field. A gleaming monstrosity of mirrored glass amidst the three or four floor concrete boxes. She guessed it must be fourteen floors at least, not a big deal at home but easily the tallest building she had seen in Aetalus. Ivan took them down a series of side streets, so the tower would come into view only to be lost again, eventually leading them into another building.

"If we approach directly then we will draw the attention of the guards," he said. "For now, we must be circumspect in the approach, as other scavenger parties are. The Stewards do not like non-residents coming too close to their home. As well, remember that we are still seeking supplies to return with, we must do our job as well as complete the studies you wish to undertake. I think from the top floor you should be able to see the tower and its surrounding grounds better. Ursula and I dwelt on the other side of the tower, but in a similar region of the community, and I feel this building will provide a similar view."

Cassidy thanked him as they made their way to the fourth floor and found a window that gave a good vantage of the tower grounds and lower floors of the tower itself. Ivan left her at the window while he searched the room.

"I will search the other dwellings in this building while you examine the tower," he told her. "Then we return to the shelter if we desire to return today. We should have time for the return trip if we only take what we find here and go back by the most direct route."

Cassidy only nodded by way of response and resumed her study, pulling a pair of binoculars from her ever-present bag. From this vantage she could see that the tower was fenced with what must have been an exceptionally tall chain link, topped by barbed wire which protruded above the snow level. There was only one gate which she could see; it seemed to be manned by a pair of guards sitting in a small guard shelter. 'Probably glorified parking lot attendants,' she thought. The land between the gate and the building was flat and open, no cover existed on the well cleared grounds, save the odd drifting of snow which she would have to crawl through if she was sneaking in. There were doors on both sides of the building which she could see. The guards inside one doorway were plain for her to see so she assumed the other entries would be guarded as well.

As she scanned the grounds again, she caught movement at the gate at the edge of her vision. Focusing on that gate, she saw a pair of figures dressed in a uniform similar to the guards stationed there. The newcomers presented papers to the guards there, then pass through the gates as they opened. She continued watching as the figures proceeded through the grounds repeating the process at the doors of the building that she couldn't make out as clearly. This confirmed her suspicion about the guards stationed there while giving her the kernel of an idea.

After a few more moments of watching the building she grew bored and turned her attention to the room she was in. Her quick search turned up a few items that may be of use, including a pair of sunglasses which she thought looked rather stylish and might help cut down the glare from the snow. Then she moved on to the other rooms in the building. Each time the room presented a view of

Steward Tower she took a moment to examine the facility for a moment before continuing with her task. With her bag filled, she returned to the building's entryway to find Ivan waiting.

"Have you completed all that you wished to?" he asked her from the chair he had settled himself on.

"I think I've done what I can, for now," she sighed. "Let's head back and let me process what I've seen." With that the pair headed back into the windy street under the cover of a swirling snowfall.

CHAPTER ELEVEN

Travelling the most direct route to the shelter meant bypassing the small stockpiles they had deposited throughout Aetalus during the day, but their route combined with the fact that they were no longer stopping to search buildings, ensured that their travel was much faster than it had been earlier in the day. Cassidy almost felt as if she were out for a stroll with a friend in the snow back on Earth, when most people would be huddled inside watching television. The scale of the architecture and her companion made her feel like she was a child walking with a parent or grandparent. She knew this world faced upheaval and hardships, but the way the snow shrouded the deserted streets in the fading light of early evening felt like returning home from a day of skiing on winter break when she was still in school.

Remembering one such day in high school when she and her friends, after a day of skiing, had talked their way into a staff retreat at the resort where they'd spent the day.

"Into that building," Ivan shouted, shoving her in the direction of the nearest open window. He whipped his atlatl out and launched his spear at something on the other side of the roadway. Cassidy plunged through the opening and looked behind her to see the man sprinting towards her. She pulled herself to one side of the window, peering behind him to see what was chasing him. On Earth she'd have called the short creature bounding towards them a rabbit, if rabbits had horns in place of floppy ears. Refusing to let such a small creature put them off the straighter line, she took out her slingshot and slipped a marble into the pouch. She rapid fired a few times, knowing that she must have hit the creature as it scampered off.

"What was that?" she gasped, slingshot held at the ready.

"That was a haribou," Ivan responded between breaths. "A common herbivore in the area, very territorial. Farmers have lost eyes to their attacks. They are an excellent source of protein, if you can kill them on the first shot."

She saw blood in the snow when she stepped back into the street. "We can't let the creature go injured like that," she said. "I have to make sure it gets the finishing stroke, edible or not. Unless haribou have doctors of some sort to patch their wounds?"

Ivan retrieved his spear and said, "No, we must make sure it does not suffer due to our clumsy hunting. Keep your shotsling ready, it cannot have gotten far after losing this amount of blood." The pair followed the combined trail of hoof prints and blood into an alley between buildings and found the creature crouched beneath a metal staircase.

Ivan crept along the opposite side of the alley, seeking

a clear shot at the diminutive haribou while Cassidy took up a guard position at the mouth of the alleyway, slingshot ready to fire at the first sign of movement from the rodent. The former engineer, foregoing the atlatl's launcher, gripped his spear underhanded as he edged towards the stairwell, then he lunged. Cassidy let loose the shot in the pouch as the creature bolted towards her. The shot flew true, felling the animal instantly, though its forward momentum carried the body forward over the icy ground. Ivan grabbed the creature by one horn, tying the haribou to one of the straps of his carrysac.

"It is good that this detour was not lengthy. We will still have to hurry to reach the shelter in a timely manner," Ivan said. "We must be better prepared to defend ourselves while making such speed as we can."

They resumed their journey at a brisker pace than the sauntering stroll they had been travelling at. Soon Cassidy was sweating and breathing shallowly, though the pace was not unbearable, simply taxing. Ivan settled into a loping jog and they made it back to the shelter shortly after dark.

Ivan passed the haribou to one of the fire-minders and the map to Sulva while Cassidy got them both bowls of gruel from the food line. They rushed their meals afoot while the others prepared the communal sleep area for the evening, then fell into the peaceful slumber that follows any hard labour. It was a measure of how exhausted she was that Cassidy slept the night through without awakening.

CHAPTER TWELVE

The morning found Cassidy the last still in her bedding. She shivered her way to the fire and did her best to let the warmth soak into every fibre of her being. She gratefully accepted the cup of tea and bowl of gruel she was offered, savouring each sip and bite as she warmed from the inside as well. She enjoyed the lazy morning, unsure if it was her status as an outsider or the simple fact of having been sent on procurement runs on each of the two previous days which granted her the privilege.

Breakfast eaten, dishes cleaned and returned to the appropriate stations, she ventured further into the shopping plaza, browsing through the open stores idly. In a store that specialized in hunting and hiking paraphernalia she found a knife with a blade made of a metal she had never seen before. She slipped it onto her belt, knowing that an extra knife can always come in handy. In another store she found goods that left her puzzled; she inspected each of the items she found there but could make no sense of them, 'Maybe a toy store,' she thought after finding what was definitely stuffed haribou and cineleucia lined up on a shelf. It was nice to see the reminder that all societies had some form of cuddling toy for their young. Another shop turned out to have a variety of things which were clearly musical instruments; she might not have recognized many of them but a drum was always plainly a drum it seemed. There were also stores which had specialized in jewelry, all of those had been emptied either by looters or to pay off the families in the early days.

Her wandering finally took her through all that the plaza had had to offer before it became a shelter. She found that many of the shops had been converted for varying purposes. The central area had become the dominant focal point for the residents, where the main fire and cook fire were kept burning and where they slept communally. A news agent had been converted into a reading lounge; what she assumed had once been the food court had become a sort of workshop where they exercised skills like sewing and weaving to generate more clothing and bedding. She found that the kitchen area of the largest vendor in the food court had been transformed to process the animals the group caught, and was told that the hides were tanned in a nearby building, to prevent the smell from becoming unbearable for those in residence. The biggest shock to her was to find that despite the lack of electricity they still had running water and shower facilities. Further inquiry let her discover that she could have a long cold shower today or a short warm shower in two days time when the group would build larger fires in the water heaters. The archaeologist in her decided a quick shower was in order now, with a warm shower to follow when permitted.

She managed to rinse the worst of the grime from

her body before the cold became unbearable, then shivered her way reluctantly into grimy clothing. She decided it was time to find herself some clean clothes while she pondered the problem of the tower some more. But first, tea. While she sipped, she attempted to read some of the children's books she found in the book store. The written language seemed close to English but in an odd script, the images of familiar items with the equivalent of "B is for Ball" allowed her to grasp the rudiments of the local lingo. Hopefully she could pick up enough to manage to navigate the community on her own.

As pleasant as it was to spend the day with little to worry about, the problems she would face when she returned home were on her mind. How would she deal with her current work situation, unless she demanded some form of payment from Gamgee to at least help with her rent? The absences from the university could only be explained as research trips for so long before they began to see some portion of the results from those trips. If she couldn't come up with a workable plan to face those problems then there was no reason to return. With those thoughts in her head she drifted into an unsettled sleep, and dreamt of wolves in three-piece suits chasing her.

She awoke from her nap as the scavenger teams were returning for the day and quickly corned Flavius to grill him for information about the tower. "Well, all I ever saw was the delivery docks in the back," he said. "And maybe the washrooms once or twice, but I couldn't swear to that. I remember it was always a big to-do: show your id at the gate on the way in; show it at the loading dock while they unloaded the truck. I didn't like that part so much;

letting them into the truck seemed wrong somehow. Then I'd have to show my id again on the way out with a receipt for the delivery."

"That seems almost paranoia level of security," Cassidy said.

"Well, they were dealing with some sensitive equipment so I guess they'd want to be extra safe with that stuff. I had to get special clearance just to be allowed on the trucks driving the deliveries," he said. "Plus, they probably had all kinds of orders for safety from the government and from the companies building the devices. Wouldn't want just anybody being able to make their own, now would you?"

"What were you delivering anyway?"

"Parts usually. They can't make everything they need at all the towers so a lot of the parts were trucked from one tower to another. One trip they sent me from Stewards to Marshalls Tower—Marshalls Tower is about four hundred ells north of here by the way," he said. "Not a long haul by itself, but knowing they had armed guards in the back of my truck didn't make me feel very comfortable. 'Course they didn't always send armed guards with the parts, that was for the power core or something like that, a really expensive piece."

"Armed guards with a delivery sounds a bit extreme," replied Cassidy. "Even if the cargo is expensive."

The delivery driver thought for a moment. "It was, and there was no street escort to go along with it. I just remember it being something they were determined to get to Marshalls. That was only the one time though, usually it was just making sure I signed in and out properly."

"Who else here might have delivered to the towers?"

"Sulva did. Just about any of the other veteran scouts really; most of us were short range or long-haul delivery and most of the deliveries here were for the tower or from there," he answered.

Cassidy made a point of interviewing all the scouting crews. Everybody who had delivered to the tower reported the same. Sulva did report that when she had delivered an official from one of the other families, that guest was ushered in while she was turned back to the gate.

"He was taken in like he belonged there and I was sent on. I hear he left a few days later by whichever courier happened to be stopping there; was kind of hoping to get the job myself because it was easier than the normal milk runs with multiple deliveries. He was just straight from tower to tower," the driver told Cassidy.

While she had been given the day to relax, Cassidy was not given the full day of doing nothing. After the evening meals were served, she was put to work with the cleaning crew. Her task for the day was to carry water to the fires to be heated, then return the water for use in the kitchens in the food court. Not an onerous task, but not light work either. Still she preferred it to actually washing the dishes. 'Who likes washing dishes?' she wondered. 'I guess folks who don't do it that often might like it as a novelty. The kind of folks who live in high towers and get special treatment from courier services.'

CHAPTER THIRTEEN

The next morning, she was sent out with a new party. They made the way to what Cassidy instinctively called north in the community, repeating the process she had gone through with Ivan two days previously. This area of the community had been little checked she learned, it was largely residential and they had been focusing on the more commercial and industrial areas out of respect for their fellow citizens, but now months into the troubles they were beginning to have less hope that anybody would be able to return for their personal possessions.

Her carrysac was bulging when she found the key to the idea which had been in the back of her mind. An older uniform for one of the tower engineers, a little big for her but hopefully somebody at the shelter could resize it to fit her. She crammed the outfit into her own bag and continued the pattern the team had been following, finding a new carrysac to take the remaining supplies she found.

As they began their return journey, she held her slingshot at the ready, as she had at all points when they were in the open; between her own efforts and those of her fellows, they had already felled several small animals to bring back to the shelter. She was unsure if she was hoping for more prey or simply worried about running into another cineleucia. But the only other creatures they saw were birds flying in the far distance.

Shifting the weight of the carrysac on her back, Cassidy looked about the alleyway where the group had paused for a break. In the back of the alley she spotted what looked like table legs emerging from the snow. Closer inspection, and some snow clearing, revealed a small table.

"We've got plenty of firewood back at the shelter," one of the others said when she rejoined the group, dragging the table behind her.

"It's not for wood," she said while tying a piece of rope to two of the now upright table legs. Then, dropping her carrysac and bag onto the flat portion of the table, she signalled her readiness to proceed. Just as she had hoped, the small table slid over the hard-packed snow like a sleigh. Occasionally it would catch in a wind-blown ridge of the snow, but such obstacles were typically easily overcome by simply pulling a little harder.

"You look like a caballa," the one who had insisted they needed no more firewood said. "But it seems to make the journey easier."

"I'm not sure what a caballa is but we used similar things where I come from; when the snow was too deep for wheels, we'd put skis on carts to make them into sleighs," she said. "They make carrying loads much easier than just piling it all your back."

"I don't know what skis are but if it means you can glide over the snow, I'd like to try them," he said.

Her going was much easier after that, despite the additional weight her team mates added to her small sleigh, and soon the entire crew had similarly outfitted themselves with improvised sleighs yoked together with whatever strings they could find in the buildings they passed. They began retrieving items from the small stockpiles they had built on their outward journey and had soon doubled their loads, thrilled to be bringing a much larger quantity of goods back to the shelter than they had initially expected.

They were greeted at the entrance to the shopping plaza with shock and joy. The introduction of the sleds was welcomed with enthusiasm and immediate plans for how to improve the primitive devices for use among the engineers who were still learning how to deal with the snow months after it had begun to fall. She did a quick sketch of a toboggan for them, explaining the practical and recreational uses of the simple device.

Later, cup of tea in hand, Cassidy watched the early results of their experiments. She was still amazed that while they had such advanced technology in some regards, they had large gaps in their knowledge compared to Earth. Of course, it could be a simple case of both this region and those who dwelt here being below the normal snowline. With these thoughts in mind, she dug out the tower uniform she had found earlier and began to inspect it.

Ursula, seeing her with the uniform, came over. "What are you doing with that?"

Cassidy looked up, "I'm not sure yet, but I think it might help me get into the tower. I think if I disguise myself as somebody who works there, I could just walk in at shift change."

"It's a good idea, except everybody who works at Steward Tower lives there," the short Tellan answered. "The same as at all the other towers. That was on one of the last news reels, all the important and necessary staff were being resettled within tower confines to keep them running and protect the weather dominators."

Cassidy, who had been feeling like she had accomplished much that day, looked at the dark-haired girl, crestfallen. "Then I guess this just goes in the bins to clothe whoever it'll fit. I still need to find a way into the tower. I can't leave here without trying to at least get you folks out of this ice age. Besides Doctor Gamgee will be furious if I come back empty-handed."

Ursula laid a hand on the itinerant archaeologist's shoulder, and the pair sat quietly for a moment. "What if we pretended to be from one of the other towers?" she asked. "We'd need another uniform, but two guards travelling with a message for Steward sounds like something that could happen, especially if the towers are having as much trouble with their radios as we are."

Cassidy lit up, "We could even just claim to be looking for parts to fix the radio, or some part of the tower. Just about anything to get through the doors, and then I can deal with whatever is inside. Guess we need to go chat with Ivan, unless you can think of anybody else with inside experience?"

Ursula sighed heavily, "I'm still not ready to face him, but if you must then I hope you will do it on your own. I'll make another of those shot-slings you showed me; those would be handy in any situation."

"I'll hold off on that for a little while, I think we need

to explore a little more to see if we can find another uniform. Hopefully one that will fit either you or me better than this one does," Cassidy said. "At least we now have some idea of how we can proceed."

The trio ate their evening meal while quietly adding to their plans. After the meal Ursula gathered materials from the various shops in the plaza to make more sling shots for the group while Cassidy sought out what she thought of as a phone book but was informed was called a community directory, to find potential dwellings where another uniform could be found.

After her search proved fruitless, Cassidy split her remaining waking hours between helping with the sleighs and building more of the primitive weapons she had introduced to this world—so like her own, yet so different than her home. Then she slept the sleep of the just and very tired, glad that she now had some idea of her next step. The cycle of a day of activity followed by a day of rest now seeming routine.

After a solid night of sleep and a rushed breakfast of full rations, she set out on her own in the morning. Searching all the nearby buildings she failed to find a uniform, never mind one near her size; her undersized stature for this world was more hindrance than simply being thought underaged, it seemed. She was about to give up on the plan entirely when she found what she thought would be a perfect solution in a dress bag in the back of a closet of the penthouse suite of a nearby apartment building. It would be one of the least practical outfits she had seen on this world, with the exception of the swimming attire left untouched in the shopping plaza, but might be the perfect thing for her subterfuge. 'This might even make it more believable,' she said to the empty room before she slipped the clothing into her bag and made her way back to the street just as darkness was falling.

She made her way slowly towards the shelter, nervous about being alone in the gathering darkness. Slingshot at the ready, despite the fact that she could barely see where she was going, she wished her cell phone still had some charge left so that she would have some light available for the return journey. Instead she counted the intersections as she passed them, hoping that she would remember the way and not make a wrong turning somewhere in the dark.

Eventually though she gave up on the journey. She could not read the street signs in the dark, could barely decipher them and their still unfamiliar writing in the daylight if she were honest with herself, and while she could usually manage to match the symbols on the road signs with those on the map she had been provided when she went on salvage mission, she couldn't read that by the light of the half moon in the sky. Ducking into the first building she saw, she made herself a makeshift nest in the first open room she found and prepared for a cold, hungry, sleepless night.

A quick search of the small room she had chosen revealed a small supply of candles and some drinking glasses. Relieved, she used her new knife to cut the base of the candles off so that they would fit into the glasses and made herself a travel lantern. Knowing she would be late to the shelter but determined to get there anyway, she returned to the street. A quick study of the nearest sign with a comparison to her map showed her to be less than three streets away from the shelter. That meant she had been more turned around than she had thought: she'd gone little more than a block that day, thinking that what she wanted would probably not have been taken by anybody out scavenging for the surviving groundlings. Relieved to be back on track, she did not notice the scurrying sounds that grew louder until the first of the crocuta nearly tripped her.

Then she saw the mass running towards her, a convulsing carpet of the roughly-furred forms rippling in the light of her lantern. The grey and black and brown furred forms clawed their way over each other and past her with the force of a river in spring flood as Cassidy did her best to stay upright and let them pass while wondering what could have caused the small creatures to stampede through the roadway. When the tide had slowed to a trickle and she had found her feet she looked ahead to see a flickering orange glow reflected on the low cloud cover.

She broke into a sprint towards the glow, slowing only to confirm her direction at larger street crossings, grateful for the hard-packed surface the frequent traffic had made of the snow as she hurried towards what she hoped was not the disaster she feared. The wind brought the smell of smoke to her nose, at first just enough to be aware of before becoming strong enough to hamper her breathing. Eyes streaming, she pressed onwards into the growing light. Soon she could see flames had engulfed one of the low structures just this side of the shopping plaza. The heat of the blaze made it nearly impossible for her to continue along her current route.

Dashing to a side street, she quickly found herself in a narrow alley littered with refuse from the shelter. Discarded bedding and food scraps making walking treacherous, she slowed somewhat but proceeded as swiftly as she could, the sounds of screaming and shouting reaching her ears from the general direction of the fire. She increased her speed and pushed on until she came to a fence. Refusing to turn back and seek any other way to the shelter, she began climbing the obstacle and had just reached the top when a gate swung open with her on it.

Below her passed three figures dressed in the mottled greys and blacks she thought of as a night camouflage pattern. Cassidy clutched the top of the gate like a shipwrecked sailor might grasp a plank in the sea, staring down at the group. The rearmost of the strangely clad figures dropped something as it reached behind and swung the gate firmly shut with a clang only slightly muffled by the figure atop it. She waited until they were out of sight and then counted slow to thirty, just to be sure they were gone, before dropping back to the ground. Torn between following the strangers and going to the aide of her new friends, she opted to give assistance where she could and, opening the gate, resumed her rush to the shelter.

As she rounded the last corner between her and the shelter, she felt the heat of the fire crash into her like a charging bull, forcing the air from her lungs. She gasped in a mouthful of smoke and began coughing, but pressed on to the first group of people she saw. The blazing building, which seemed to be one of the residences neighbouring the shopping plaza, showed Flavius, Sulva, and Ursula guiding people away from the blaze while others were throwing snow at the flames, trying to smother or drown the conflagration. With only a slight hesitation, she rushed to the line of fleeing refugees, calling to Ursula as she approached.

"We need to get everybody somewhere counter to the wind," the dark-haired woman said. "There's a pre-planned alternate shelter a short distance from here, where we're bringing the elders and younglings, but some of these people will need help to reach it. Can you help them? Take their carrysacs, or just keep them from falling too far behind."

Cassidy nodded and ran to aide a wobbly older man, lending him a shoulder to use for stability and taking his carrysac alongside her own. They followed the pro-gression of other folks to the alternate shelter, a building which reminded her of a bank. Once there Cassidy saw to it that the man got inside, then turned back to help ferry the next likely pilgrim to the new shelter.

She repeated the process several times until, barely able to lift her feet, she returned to the shopping plaza and found that only those actively fighting the blaze remained. She joined Ursula in a line of people passing bucketfuls of snow toward the fire.

"We're keeping it contained but can't put it out with-out accessing the fire fighting equipment," the young en-gineer told her. "Father was supposed to be getting that back into working order."

Cassidy nodded in reply, too exhausted to use words. Her arms already tightening from the effort of helping people from the old to the new shelter, were finding the simple effort of passing the buckets up the line harder and heavier with each new load. After what felt like thousands of repetitions, she heard shouts of joy coming from the direction of the fire. Looking up, she noticed three things simultaneously.

The sky was lightening as the sun rose. The fire was beginning to falter under the onslaught of those fighting it. Water was streaming into the blaze.

"Ivan got the hose systems working!" Ursula shouted with joy. The brigade of bucketeers took the opportunity to pause, but soon resumed their work. Seeing the end in sight, they passed the fuller buckets along the line faster than before. They fought the fire for what felt like hours before Cassidy finally stumbled from the line and collapsed into the snow.

CHAPTER FOURTEEN

Cassidy awoke uncertain of where she was. She looked around, seeing that she was rolled in bedding on a smooth stone floor, near a fire. As awareness returned, she remembered the events of the previous evening and recognized the building she had seen in the brief moments while she delivered people to the new shelter.

She rose slowly and walked to the main fire on legs that simultaneously refused to bend or support her. Every muscle in her body aching, she collapsed onto a chair and croaked, "Tea? Water?"

The first gentleman she had escorted to the new shelter gestured for her to stay where she was and soon made his way to her, leaning on a short cane. "Thank you," he said. "You helped so much last night."

"Did we succeed?" Cassidy asked. "Did we manage to save the old shelter?"

The older man sat next to her. "They managed to extinguish the blaze but not before it had spread somewhat. The fire had started on the shelter and wind carried it to a neighbouring building. The shelter was lost before you had returned from your expedition." Seeing the shocked look on her face he hurried on. "Not destroyed, but one wall was burnt too badly for us to stay there and stay warm. The plan right now is to send a group back to re- trieve whatever can be salvaged later today."

"At least there was this building to use," Cassidy said. "How did you manage to get it sorted so quickly?"

"When it became apparent that the shelters might be- come long term dwellings it was decided to prepare alter- nates," the man said. "It was something many of us fought at first—why split our resources when keeping them all together was easier to manage? That was the thought of those who refused to leave their homes at first, too. Then the families cut the electricity and we knew that we'd have to take shelter together, save those few who remembered how to live independently. When even those folks started coming to the shelters warning of the increased blizzards and higher winds coming, some went out and prepared these alternates. This one has better ventilation for the fire, but not as good resources for everything else. But it will do for now. I worked in this counting-house, while such business still mattered, before the families closed all the branches in favour of central houses only. My son always joked that I should just live here because I spent so much time at work," he chuckled.

"I'm just glad we're all someplace warm," Cassidy an- swered, then, thanking him for the warm drink, she went off to find Ursula and Ivan, to see what the plan for re- trieving the things from the old shelter would be.

They all waited until the next day, those most able- bodied making the trip back to the shopping plaza to re- trieve whatever they could. "How did the fire start on the wall furthest from the fire?" Ursula asked as she inspected the damage. "There is simply no way I can imagine that the wind spread the fire to the opposite side of the building, especially not considering where it spread after that."

"The night of the fire I had a near miss with some folks I thought might have been bad news," Cassidy began, then related the events of the alleyway.

"I think I know the place but can you take us there?" Sulva asked. At a nod from Cassidy they trooped out into the cold. Cassidy led them to the gate, pointing out where she had fallen and other landmarks she could recognize in the daylight. There wasn't much to see after the recent snowfalls, but a little digging uncovered a container that the locals recognized as a common fire starter.

As they returned to the shopping plaza to finish collecting what they could, the group discussed the situation. "Somebody set the fire; we won't find the tracks now but this is really all the proof we need," Ivan said. "We shall have to carry this news back to the counting-house. They will most likely institute exterior guards now, in addition to the fire-minders. The retrieval teams will be shorted in numbers due to this."

Ursula looked at the container in her hand. "Yes, it was deliberately set, but who would do it? We haven't seen any other refugees in months and most of them came into our party when we moved in here." She finished piling items onto her makeshift sleigh and tied the stack down.

"There were signs of others in some of our stock houses from time to time," Sulva said. "Used candles, missing goods, little things like that we figured were miscounted or one of the other teams used them while they were out. But never any major changes or damages. Do you really think that the Stewards would send out attackers?"

The group looked at each other wordlessly. Their silence held while they finished tying their respective loads to the sleighs and made their way to the new shelter.

CHAPTER FIFTEEN

Though it had taken all of the capable the full day, most of the supplies made their way to the counting-house shelter. Including Cassidy's guard outfit. With the knowledge that the tower was now attacking the refugees, at least their camp, Cassidy decided that she could no longer delay.

Over the previous days she had been quietly sounding out those who the guard uniform might fit, searching for an accomplice for her planned undercover mission. Cassidy had decided to disguise herself as a ranking, but junior, member of one of the other tower families. She would take with her a scientist and an armed guard to act as chaperones while she went to retrieve some component needed to repair her home tower. Once inside the Steward Tower they would hopefully turn off the machinery, hopefully returning normal weather to this portion of the planet.

She approached Ursula and gave her the outlines of the plan, explaining that she would need somebody who not only understood the technology but could pass as somebody who would be sent on such mission as escorting the brat of the family on an outing. The engineer practically leapt at the opportunity, saying that they would need to visit her former dwelling to get some supplies.

The pair then approached Sulva, who responded with a simple, "Yeah, sure. Beats letting them freeze us to death or burn us out of our shelters. Besides I was known to carry items between towers anyway; if anybody remembers me, they'd just congratulate me on the promotion." The trio spent the rest of the evening discussing the plan while Cassidy adjusted the uniform she had found so that it would fit the former delivery driver.

The next day the trio made their way to the dwelling Ursula had occupied before the troubles started. "It was not a great dwelling, but it was all I could afford on a student's stipend," the engineer said. "I had intended to move when I was a bit more established in my work, but the troubles..." she trailed off.

In Cassidy's eyes it could have been any of the more luxurious studio-style apartments she had occupied on Earth, both as a student and since graduating. The furniture, while not new, was in better shape than much of what she had seen in most places during her time as a scavenger, in better shape than anything she had owned herself. "This is a really nice apartment," she said.

"Much nicer than most of the places I've lived since I moved here," Sulva said. "I'd almost like to convert this into a dwelling for us three. Just take a little vacation and let them all deal with things for a little while."

Ursula shushed them while she went about collecting her gear. Cassidy thought that her plan might be more than a little silly on the costuming side, given that they'd all have to maintain their scavenged exterior clothing, but insisted that they maintain whatever scant cover they could.

Cassidy looked out the window: they were on the fourth floor of the building and it granted them a wider view than most buildings she had been in. Through the snow, in the direction she considered north, she could see the streets laid out in a mathematically perfect grid, each intersection razor sharp. Most of the blocks she could see were snowclad blocks, peaceful in the white blankets. Some blocks, obviously intended as park spaces for the members of Aetalus, were blankets of snow with skeletal trees protruding from the uniform sheets, lending a quilt-like appearance to the city. The squared geometry echoing street after street, roadway after roadway, a monument to urban planning and development, felt sinister in its lack of organic growth; the blanket of snow amplifying. A city meant to support a machine, the people dwelling there an afterthought, cogs and gears to drive society. Not living members of the group, rather functional blocks to hold things rigid in the now twisted permanent winter that faced those outside the tower she pictured rising like a hissing serpent behind her to the south. A small part of her wondered what kind of people could do this to each other, while another part reflected that this could easily happen on Earth if the technology was realized there.

She didn't have to try very hard to picture the type of people who would fund such a mad science project, and they looked suspiciously like those she saw on the business news every day. The politicos who stumped all the posts for their favourite candidates and slung the mud at their opponents in the name of filling their own pockets. The same as the people she saw on the news everyday denying that climate change was happening on Earth so that the companies they invested in could continue to profit. Earth might not have the families, to the best of her knowledge, but it definitely had clans who attempted to run things in the same way. The conglomerates just hadn't gained a strong enough foothold to stand upon the throats of those they saw as being beneath them yet. 'Maybe I should just leave the device here,' she thought. 'I don't think that there's anybody who would use something like this in any better manner at home.'

It wasn't until the cityscape before her started to blur that she realized she was weeping. Weeping for the world she had come to, and the one she had left behind.

CHAPTER SIXTEEN

The three made their way back to the shelter of the counting-house without event, arriving with plenty of daylight left they began sorting the items they would need for their expedition to the tower. It took a full day of sewing but soon they had their disguises complete and decided to set out at the first opportunity.

The next day dawned under a furious blizzard. The highest windows showing only white, the trio hunkered down near one of the doorways with one of the tourism guides for the tower. Ivan, himself at a loss as to how best spend his time, approached them.

"What has the three of you so intimate today?" he asked in his curiously accented manner.

Ursula looked up from where she sat and said, "We are planning to infiltrate the tower. We're trying to learn the layout of the floors we might have access to."

The aging engineer blinked owlishly. "I had thought you would have been gone by now," he said. "May I add my knowledge to that you have already?"

At a nod from Cassidy he began sketching further diagrams on the building plan the group had been studying, making notations in the margins of how things had been arranged when he had last worked in the tower. "They cannot have changed the architecture of the tower substantially since I worked there; all of the basic machinery must remain in their operational parameters. The structure of the management has probably changed significantly though. When I worked there last it was Madame Steward, but I think she has passed and her son Sage is now the head of the tower: it is the head of the Steward family who will have the absolute authority to allow you to stay or force you to leave. He was little more than a boy when I met him, and friendly in his manner, but to let this go on as it has, he must have grown up to become a very different man."

"Thank you for this," Cassidy said. "Anything else you can tell us that might make this go any easier?"

He scratched his beard before pointing to two places on the map he had added his own notes to. "Here is where you will find the master circuit joiner; if you disable this then no power will flow to the device. This other is the main console; from there you can change the weather between here and the nearest towers. But the towers must be balanced, simply turning off the device here will see the normal weather of this region return but tempered by the others."

"Like standing between two heat sources when neither is close enough to provide adequate warmth?" Ursula enquired in an academic voice.

"Yes, but in our case, it will be between cold source and other cold source," Ivan elaborated. "We will not return to the typically humid weather we had before, instead it will become temperate unless the other towers are adjusted likewise."

The quartet sat in silence for a moment while they let this sink in, then Cassidy spoke, "The best we can do right now is attend to the tower at hand. After that we can think on how to broaden the reach, maybe boost this tower's signal or send a team to another tower. Who knows? But step one is the Steward Tower."

"I will consider on the matter while you three take your action," the older engineer said simply. "I simply wished for you to all know the best possible outcome of your action, and to add what assistance I could. I fear there will be too many who remember me within the tower for me to be of any other assistance."

The rest of the day passed under a cloud of nervous energy. The team packed their bags, then unpacked them, shuffling the items they felt they would need, replacing items at random. Sulva commented that they would know what they needed when the situations arose and the best they could do was guess.

Cassidy decided to keep the equipment she had carried when she came through this slip, plus the clothing she had acquired on planet. She had seen herself through so many situations with similar basic equipment, plus she had added the slingshot, which was good for some fun if nothing else. That decided, she settled herself into the routine of checking her gear, sharpening her blades, and packing the bag as light as she could manage. It would be a lengthy trek and those didn't vary much from planet to planet and always ended with the feeling of walking too far with too much weight. Ursula followed Cassidy's lead, selecting similar items to those the archaeologist would carry, selecting the atlatl over the slingshot. "I'm more skilled with it and it doesn't take much more space," she explained. Sulva's bag was mostly food and clothing, though the tough woman carried both an atlatl and a slingshot.

A few days later, when the weather had cleared enough for travel, they set out for the tower. Working their way through the city, first in a dominantly eastern direction with slight southward tendencies, the group saw no signs of life. In fact, they saw little movements beyond the eddies of snow that formed in some of the intersections on the street; the snow dervishes lashed them with sharp ice particles, sometimes necessitating choosing alternate routes.

"The winds seem more intense than yesterday," Ursula observed.

Cassidy, finally growing tired of her stay in Aetalus pushed them onwards. Further from the shelter and only marginally closer to the tower, as they had agreed. They intended to approach the Steward Tower from the rough direction of the Joplin Tower to lend greater believability to their story of being emissaries of Joplin Tower. They pushed on until the winds rose and more snow started falling, then sought shelter in the first building they could gain access to. They huddled together for warmth in the small room they had chosen, burning what they could find in a small metal garbage can Sulva had found in the building.

The next day was a repeat of the previous one, heading more south than the previous day. Another day without incident, and another night in a random building. This time, unable to build a fire, they gathered what coverings they could and built a nest of all the cushions and mattresses they could find in the rooms of the building they had settled on.

Their third day out from the shelter brought them to the entrance of the tower late in the day, tired, cold, and hungry. Cassidy presented her credentials, which identified her as Cassidy Joplin, daughter of Scott and Janis Joplin of the Joplin Tower family. She and her companions were granted admittance to the Steward Tower as ambassadors of the families.

CHAPTER SEVENTEEN

The security team had taken a look at the documents Ursula had prepared and sent the trio into a private room three floors above the ground. There they had been met by a young lady who asked their names and positions before requesting their credentials and, after separating them from their meagre belongings, sent them a further three floors higher.

On the sixth floor they were met by a Nancy Raigin, who told them that for the duration of their stay in the Steward Tower she would be their guide. "The Lord Steward has had a trying time governing the surrounding regions and is not accepting callers at this moment, but will arrange to see you in future days," the official told them. "In the meantime, we request that you refresh yourselves and enjoy all that we have to offer. Anything you require can be supplied by those who work within this tower, one of the harmonious thirteen as prescribed by the great technocrats who preceded the establishment of this glorious age."

Cassidy and Ursula, as those pretending to be the representatives of the neighbouring tower, voiced their acceptance. Meanwhile Sulva made a show of inspecting the room to which they had been assigned. The small group settled into the luxurious suite they had been provided with, enjoying the stark contrast to the horrible cold they had left behind in comparison to the warmth of the temperate room with which they had been provided.

Their well-heated room featured a bed for each of them, twin beds for the scientist and guard but a full-sized queen for the representative of the tower family. Each bed was in a separate room under its own climate control. Despite the luxury offered them the trio slept together in the queen-sized bed, their combined history of huddling together for warmth making them feel more comfortable if they stayed together in an easily defensible unit. They even took watches throughout the night, Sulva taking first and last watch in their four-watch division.

Despite the undisturbed evening, none of them slept well. The combination of finally having infiltrated their goal and the shock of relative comfort versus the hardships they had faced making it to their destination, left all of them on edge, not allowing their adrenaline to dissipate to the point of letting any of them find true rest. They each luxuriated in the hot shower provided in the en suite bathroom and gorged themselves on the food which a nameless tower employee brought to their room. Cassidy felt like she was in an all-inclusive five-star resort back on Earth, the view making her think they'd all be hitting the slopes on snowboards or skis the next day. After a suitable time had elapsed for a very lazy morning under any circumstances there came a knock at their door.

"I hope all is well with you," Nancy said when Sulva

opened the door. "I understand that your travels must have been difficult so it has been decided that today we will conduct you on a tour of the tower, so that any dissimilarities between ours and your own will not become problematic. Unfortunately, the Lord Steward is still unable to accept guests as he manages the current situation with regards to the debtors." After a dramatic pause the tower representative continued, "Let us not focus on negative aspects of our current situations and instead allow you to see the new tower you have chosen to visit."

"Please allow us to dress appropriately for the outside," Cassidy responded before quickly retreating to her chamber. "We have been many days travelling with limited recourses so we beg you to bear with us in our difficult times. The roads between us were practically impassable in places, and we have had to abandon much of what we set out with."

"Indeed," Nancy responded. "It is sad that the law-abiding citizens have been forced to suffer the same punishments as those who choose to ignore those laws, but that is not a matter for us to discuss. Let us proceed when you are ready."

As Cassidy emerged from the chamber which the trio had shared, she saw others gathered near the doorway in the finest attire they had managed to find before setting out on their mission. She felt they all seemed under dressed in comparison to their assigned guide who seemed as if she would be more at home in a swank restaurant while her companions were dressed to eat in a food court at the local shopping centre.

"We understand the hardships which you must have

faced in simply making your way here. We can provide everything you will need while you are here," Nancy told them. "Today is simply to make you feel more comfortable in our tower while we arrange for the replacement mechanisms you have been sent to retrieve. When you are ready, we will begin the tour. We do our best to maintain the schedule of events here in the Steward Tower."

The three former refugees quickly grabbed their jackets and followed Nancy into the corridor. "This area of the tower, as you now know, is dedicated to visiting dignitaries. It is seldom used since the camaraderie came to rule, but is maintained regularly to be prepared for such as you who brave the isolation outside. During the construction the portion of the building dedicated to visitors was much larger." Nancy maintained a monologue as they walked through corridor after corridor, most dedicated to private chambers or public spaces.

Cassidy did her best to memorize the route they took and locations of interest, but after seeing a dozen themed sitting rooms on the three floors they were shown she asked, "Where do you house the equipment for which the towers were built?"

"In the standard positions, some on the upper floors, others on lower floors," Nancy responded. "They will not be part of this tour."

"I would very much like the opportunity to see the mechanisms in use here to compare them with those in our home tower," Ursula said. "Compare wear patterns on the frequently used components any variations in."

"They will not be part of this tour," Nancy repeated in an annoyed voice before continuing in a soothing tone.

"Here to the left you will see the ballroom where dances are conducted every Saturday evening, attendance is
mandatory. Fortunately for you this is one of the weeks
featuring live music; perhaps you would like to hear them
rehearse?"

The manner in which she asked made it clear that any
answer other than yes would not be accepted so Sulva
asked, "We have no live music in our tower, may we?"

A nod from Cassidy was echoed by Nancy and the
small group entered a lavishly appointed room. A grouping of chairs and small tables were laid out around a large,
hardwood dance floor. The walls were papered with a
purple velvet-like material which, while making the room
feel dark, did little to counteract the large chandeliers
which hung from the ceiling. At one end of the room was
a small stage, and to one side was a short bar with several bottles behind it. On stage was a four-piece act who
started playing as soon as they walked through the door.
Cassidy was as amused by their timing as she was to find
that she recognized the tune. True the lyrics were different, but if she sped it up slightly it was a song that had
once been popular on Earth.

After their, seemingly, impromptu private concert, the
group were shown the shopping district and guided back
to their rooms with the assurance that the Lord Steward
would see them at his earliest convenience and that Nancy would be at their beck and call. "Tomorrow you have
been scheduled to see the education facilities that we have
in the tower and the food production areas," the guide
told them. "Your meals will be brought to you at the appropriate time. Please enjoy your evening."

"We're supposed to just stay in our rooms?" Sulva asked as the door closed behind Nancy. She opened the door, finding Nancy nearby. "Can we see more of the tower, perhaps visit one of the public spaces?"

"You may, with a proper guide to ensure you do not get lost," Nancy said in her calmly professional voice. "It is the end of my work day; I will have somebody sent to escort you."

"There are signs showing the way, I'm certain we could make our way to the viewing gallery we passed when we returned to our rooms," Cassidy began.

"Normally we do not allow visitors to travel without escorts suitable to their station. But, of course, yes you may travel freely within the tower so long as you agree to follow all posted signage concerning who may enter selected areas," Nancy responded. "We do hope you will follow these regulations, and not hesitate to ask assistance from any passer-by should you require it."

Upon their agreement to those terms Nancy led them to the nearest public area where they were allowed to peruse a small selection of books and given access to what looked to Cassidy like one of the radios that would have been common on Earth in the 1940s. Nancy went on her way after explaining that the radionic unfortunately only received the broadcast from the tower, but that there was another one available in the sitting room of their suites should they desire to return to their own rooms. They thanked her; Cassidy turned to the window, while Ursula immediately began browsing the bookshelves, and Sulva turned on the radionic.

"What do we do next?" Cassidy asked.

Ursula held a finger to her lips as the radionic began to make faint crackling noises which slowly resolved into a male voice announcing the social events planned for the next few days. "Listeners can listen both ways," the engineer said in hushed tones as she drew closer to the archaeologist. "It's always best to assume that they are listening to us when the radionic is not being listened to."

Cassidy looked back at her with a confused expression, and Sulva cut in, "They can be made so that those on the other side hear us, like somebody staring in a window. This floor was intended to be for the use of those visiting from other families, so it would probably be best to assume all of the radionics can listen to us as well."

"It's been so long since I've seen a working one that I had forgotten about that trick, until she specified that these only received one broadcast," Ursula said. "Equipping them to listen often requires removing much of their capabilities to receive signals. It was a ploy many of the families had begun using to record what was happening in many places before they decided to freeze us into submission."

"Many governments at home used similar tactics for varying reasons," Cassidy responded. Reflecting that the Steward Tower was heightening her paranoia, she made a note to check her offices and phone when she returned home, not that she had any real reason to suspect she would be on a watch list for anybody. "Let's just enjoy the view and small entertainments they've provided for us; did I see wine on that sideboard?"

Sulva responded while inspecting the tray of drinks, "There seems to be a variety of juices, plus the makings for tea and coffee. I have not had any papple juice in far too long, want some?" A nod from Ursula told Cassidy that she should have glass as well.

The juice was chilled, pulpy like orange juice, but the closest comparison in taste she could make was a mixture of pear and plum; it was deliciously sweet after the days of drinking only the bitter tea or plain water available in the shelter. She felt a sharp stabbing pain in her back teeth, a similar sensation to an ice cream headache despite the location, and recognized it for what it was: sugar shock. She had experienced a similar pain many times on her first sip of sweetened drinks after returning from some of the more isolated digs she had been on.

"Do you not like it?" Sulva asked, seeing the newcomer wince.

"It's delicious, just surprisingly sweet," Cassidy answered with a smile and held out her empty glass. "I haven't had anything with so much sugar in a long time. May I have some more?"

Ursula, refilling their glasses, queried, "How should we proceed?"

"I am almost certain that all exits from this floor will be guarded," Sulva said, slowly sipping her papple juice. "Perhaps the best move right now is to take the opportunity to rest and study and wait to meet with the Lord Steward. It is a tactic I have had to use many times when making personal deliveries," she concluded to their puzzled looks.

"We did come to first plead our case to him. Besides, Sulva and I could use the chance to recover somewhat after the months we have spent on shorten rations and limited mobility," Ursula said quite simply. "Besides, how long could the head of the tower delay meeting representatives from another tower?"

The group looked out over the snow-covered city as the radionic switched from community announcements to a jazzy-sounding music. They remained in the seating area until serving staff summoned them to their chambers for a meal. After the meal they returned to the main bed chamber, and slept.

CHAPTER EIGHTEEN

Morning found Cassidy alone in the luxuriant room. She did some stretches and freshened her clothes from the meagre supply she had and joined the others over a tray of pastries and teas. The group were just finishing the last items on their tray when somebody knocked on their door.

Ursula mouthed "Nancy" to Cassidy as Sulva opened the door. As predicted, their guide was framed in the doorway, looking professional and entirely too perky at this time of day in Cassidy's opinion. "Are we ready to begin the scheduled activities of the day?" Nancy asked chipperly.

Cassidy, growing more used to her assumed role as leader of the delegation, said, "I believe so, but may we request a deviation from the itinerary? I feel that we could all do with some time to launder our clothing."

"But of course. I shall arrange for somebody to wash all of your garments," their host responded in her animated manner. "I will have them mend or replace any items which were damaged in your travels and we will arrange for new garments to be brought to you as well, if that is to your liking?"

A glance at the delighted faces of her companions told Cassidy all she needed to know. "That would be delightful. If we may have a moment to collect the items we desire to have cleaned, it won't take long sadly. Much of what we set out with was lost or destroyed on the journey," she concluded and gestured for her companions to follow her.

As they entered her sleeping chamber Cassidy said softly, "We need to be sure we're presentable when we finally meet the Lord Steward, and hopefully whatever they give us will be in better shape than some of what we've got." They quietly agreed while sorting their belongings to be handed off for washing. When they returned to the private sitting room with their clothing, they found Nancy and a team of serving staff waiting for them.

"I had anticipated such a request and had summoned the appropriate residents to complete these chores as I made my way to your rooms," Nancy explained with a slightly embarrassed look on her face. "Had you not been forward enough to raise the matter yourself, I would have made the offer as a matter of basic hospitality. Please forgive my tardiness in making the offer."

Cassidy did her best to reassure their host that no apology was necessary and that the situation was well sorted now. "Let us put the incident behind us and proceed, knowing that all is as it should be," the archaeologist said. After several more apologies from the guide, Cassidy prompted, "I believe that we were supposed to tour the education facilities."

The guide visibly gathered herself and quickly bustled

them off on their tour. Nancy took them to the residential corridors where she showed them various classrooms and laboratories, a small reference library, and a gymnasium which she informed them did double duty as an exercise for the younglings during school hours and adults after school had closed. "We offer educational programs for adults in neighbouring rooms, using the same facilities where possible as well," Nancy told them. "Specialized training for the operations of the tower are taught in job specific work stations."

"You don't offer simulation training for tower operation?" Ursula asked innocently.

"We offer training courses on the operations, but feel that the best way to learn such tasks is through actually performing the actions," Nancy replied simply. "Under proper supervision of course."

"Simulations are only partially accurate anyway," Sulva chimed in. "Most people learn tasks better by doing the things you're training them for."

The tour ended soon after, with Nancy escorting the group back to the sitting room on the floor where they were being housed. "Leave has been given for you to retain use of the entirety of this floor, should you so require," their guide told them. "This will include all the public areas, including the libraries, gaming areas, and lounges. Anything else you desire may be requested from any serving staff you meet."

"When we will be permitted to meet with Lord Steward?" Cassidy asked.

"Your petition has been entered into the official table of future engagements. As soon as the opportunity presents itself you will be added to the scheduled meetings for the day, regardless of how this affects the activities which have been prepared for you," Nancy said, disapproval creeping into her voice with her last sentence.

They thanked her as she left and, turning on the radionic, settled themselves on the couches nearest the window. Eventually, Cassidy rose and poured them each a measure of papple juice. As the trio listened to the broadcast from the in-tower radionic station and sipped their drinks, Cassidy noticed movement in the darkening window. Reflexively she stood, turning to look behind her, Sulva nearly mirroring her movements, which resulted in the pair ending up facing a tall man who had entered their sitting area from the hallway.

"Ah, just who I was looking for, the visiting dignitaries," the man dressed in luxurious velvety imitation of the Steward Tower livery began. "I am Chapel, the head of security and operations for this tower. I understand you have requested an audience with Lord Steward and a tour of the technical facilities. We are currently doing our best to accommodate your requests. In the meantime, I hope that your assigned guide, Domina Raigin I believe, has been keeping you all...entertained?" Cassidy nodded and the officer continued, "I simply wished to extend my personal welcome and offer my apologies for not doing so sooner. I regret that I have no further time to spare at the moment. Perhaps we will be able to meet in the near future." Here he paused dramatically, clearly waiting for some response.

Cassidy broke the silence by introducing herself and her companions. Then said, "Thank you for the gracious greetings, Chief Chapel. Everyone has been more than welcoming and everything has met our expectations. We would like to meet with the Lord Steward as soon as possible; the business of Joplin Tower depends on this meeting and our return with the items my Lord and Lady have requested."

The head of security narrowed his eyes slightly saying, "Yes, we are aware of the need which must have sent such distinguished members of the house of Joplin into such conditions as these. Unfortunately, the telegraphic communication between our towers has been inoperative for quite some time. Such excursions will no doubt become necessary more frequently in the future, but you must understand that appearing as you have, with no appointment, will require the juggling of Lord Steward's schedule significantly. Perhaps he will be able to attend the weekly festivities; normally he does not but may given the special circumstances involved. Now if you will excuse me, I do have other duties to attend to."

As the tall man strode away Cassidy gave a puzzled look to her companions, they shrugged back at her and the group returned to sipping their papple juice until the staff informed them that their meal was awaiting them in their suite. Tonight, the dish was something vegetarian, with fresh vegetables. A treat Cassidy hadn't seen since stepping through the portal. The others hadn't seen such delicacies since the snows began. They all ate ravenously.

CHAPTER NINETEEN

They were all in the sitting area of their suite drinking tea, wondering why Nancy was late, when the awaited knocking began. Mindful of their cover story, Sulva made a point of answering the door: none of them had stood on such ceremonies up to now but felt that such lax protocols may be noticed after their chat with the imposing Chief of Security Chapel the evening before.

"Hello visitors, I apologize for the lateness of my arrival today," Nancy began. "There was scheduled maintenance on the lift I normally use that I did not know of until I reached the lift itself. This required me to adjust my route. Please do not inform my superiors of my tardiness today."

Chapel spoke firmly from behind her, "There is no need to inform me of the late arrival, Nancy, I already know," he said. "And I am grateful to see it so, for I wished to accompany you for at least part of your day."

"Oh! Chief of Security Chapel," Nancy almost shrieked. "Please forgive me for not seeing you, and for my tardiness on this day. I am humbled by my failings," she concluded in a manner that suggested an often-repeated ritual.

"I am sure there is nothing to forgive," Cassidy spoke in gentle voice. "He snuck up on you and we are basically vacationing until we are granted audience with the Lord Steward."

Chapel spoke calmly in a voice clearly accustomed to shouting orders, "As long as our guests are pleased with your performance all will be well." He paused, looking pointedly at Cassidy, then continued after she gave a sharp nod, "If the House of Joplin is pleased, who am I to argue? Please, Nancy, let us proceed as scheduled."

With that settled they began a tour of the areas of the tower dedicated to food production. Their first stop looked like a large glass greenhouse to Cassidy, perhaps a little more angular than she was accustomed to, but most of her experiences with greenhouses was with the gracefully curving plastics ones which could not have withstood the heavy snowfalls which the tower itself was generating. Inside it was warmer than the simple structure would have led one to believe, even considering the strong sunshine which bathed the structure.

When asked about this, Nancy replied, "There are two systems of water-filled copper piping which radiantly heat the structure. One set of piping is bonded to portions of the power plant for the tower, serving to both heat this building and to cool the machinery which allows for the greater operation of the tower. You can see that piping running along the frames which hold the glass in place, those thin structures attached to the pipes allow for greater distribution of heat within this hothouse. The other set of piping, which does not generate as much heat, is fed by coils sunk in the lower regions of the organic refuse heaps. In this way the refuse also serves a second purpose by providing extra warmth to grow the food it is meant to become fertilizer for."

"You use the waste generated to manufacture more than the primarily desired product?" Ursula asked.

Nancy gave her a puzzled look. Then the guide looked to the chief of security and at his nod continued, "Yes, the excess heat from the steam electricity plant is fed through the entire tower in such heat-radiating devices; in the living quarters they are disguised to resemble décor, but here in a work area, they may be plainly displayed. All food and water waste that may safely be reused is composted and reused to nurture future stocks grown in the hothouses. Portions of the harvested plants grown here are given to the livestock which we are scheduled to see later today. The limits placed on us here necessitate that we use all the portions of what we produce in as many ways as we can. I have been told that this is why those who live outside the towers struggle, they don't harness all they produce and allow too much to be lost as if it were truly something to be discarded."

"Perhaps they simply do not have the means to retain all of the heat generated by an open flame. Consider how much will be held by the structure of a steam plant and what would be lost without such a structure," Ursula replied. "Many of those surviving outside the towers, the expelled, lack access to many modern conveniences."

"Surely you follow similar procedures in the Joplin Tower," Chapel inquired. "These were the guidelines established before we began the expulsion."

"We do, but a midlevel mechanical support technician would not be expected to be familiar with all the details within the tower," Cassidy improvised. "Please, do continue, our actual execution may differ from your own."

"And outside the towers is a different matter," Ursula interjected. "I have been compiling the information brought back by our patrols. Those remaining outside the towers often find themselves without comparable conditions to battle the elements. Surely this was part of the plan when the expulsion was brought into effect."

"It was indeed, and it is most of the reason my position exists within the Steward Tower," the security man said. "Though I am surprised to hear your tower still runs patrols of the surroundings, though I suppose I shouldn't be considering that Joplin Tower is located in the heart of the neighbouring capitol. We dispensed with such patrols as most of the occupants of this community were brought here specifically to work within the tower or it's pre-expulsion support industries."

Nancy interrupted, "To continue the tour, in this hothouse we have a variety of vegetables and fruits nearing the production phase of their cycles. In other houses we have earlier stages of the same plants and some others in more specialized houses. The inhabitants are encouraged to grow their own plants as well, both food crops and those for more aesthetic purposes. Unfortunately, not all the pre-expulsion crops can be grown in the hothouses, but we retain their seeds for renewal when it is decided that the snows shall be lifted."

As the guide spoke the group drifted from house to house through a series of artificially lit tunnels, eventually emerging into a hothouse the size of a baseball field. "Here is the papple orchard," Nancy spoke simply. "Right now, it is harvest time; during the rest of the season this area serves as an alternate public entertainment region, but when the papple pickers are working we only allow those employed in the task to enter. This is to ensure the safety of the workers."

The building was filled with evenly spaced trees; here and there among the trunks were benches and small electric lights. Ladders under many of the trees held workers picking the small purple fruits and placing them in baskets worn around their shoulders. Cassidy was immediately taken by the delicious smell of the fruit, quickly followed by a feeling of elation as the heightened oxygen of the building settled into her bloodstream. Feeling slightly tipsy she softly said, "We have a hothouse at home but none which hold a full orchard like this. This is truly awe-inspiring, and that can't just be the oxygen intoxication talking."

Seeing the same puzzled look on the faces of her companions, Cassidy elaborated, "When there is too much oxygen in the atmosphere it can induce a feeling of euphoria for those consuming it. This effect is often felt by those of smaller stature, those who reside at higher elevations, or those from regions where pollution is high for long periods of time. It's the direct biological opposite of elevation sickness. Surely you knew about this effect?"

"We were aware that people entering the orchard hothouse left it feeling more at peace and relaxed than when they had entered, but our research had not revealed anything of note," Nancy replied. "We assumed it was simply the beauty and stillness of the trees combined with the scent of the flowers and fruits when in season."

Ursula spoke into the silence provided by the guide's thoughtful pause, "When the trees would be at the apex of their oxygen output we should perform a test to determine if the oxygen here is indeed higher than in other places. Perhaps a simple flame test?"

The tour guide and the engineer soon devolved into a conversation so full of jargon and scientific terminology that it began to sound like gibberish to the others in the group.

"I see that the Joplins did their best to see all of their children received wide and varied educations," Chapel said.

"I travelled extensively as part of my studies, before the expulsion that is," Cassidy replied. "And studied with Professors who had not yet published their findings when the families united. It is one of the better points of coming from such notable stock."

"Indeed," the security chief said, guiding her off the path and deeper into the regularly spaced trees. "As is having the resources to build such a structure as this. I was led to believe that most scions of the tower families were raised to be little more than signatures on papers, supported by the lower levels, but this changes my opinion significantly."

Cassidy hid the thought she put into her reply by studying the tree nearest to them. "The eldest, my older siblings I mean, were taught what it was deemed important to know for running the tower. As the youngest, and least likely to ever receive any responsibility within the familiar structure, I was given more leeway in my studies. The benefit of being seen as unimportant."

"So unimportant that you appeared in none of the official portraits or at any of the public appearances?" the chief asked. "There is a Cassidy Joplin listed in the records shared among the towers, but there are no records of her appearance." Cassidy sighed inwardly at this, even knowing that this was part of the reason that Ivan had told them to select the Joplins as their alias tower. "And to arrive now, when the Joplin Tower has been silent for weeks, seeking the parts to repair a communication array. I must admit that I did have doubts originally, but if you are an imposter then you have so thoroughly set the stage for your act as to make it utterly believable."

"Then surely you will make the arrangements for us to meet with Lord Steward to request all the components we have been sent for," Cassidy said.

Chapel grinned broadly, "The more commonplace components are already being assembled and packaged for transport, along with a suitable form of transportation for one of your status. I simply wish to know what has transpired at Joplin Tower to allow it to fall into such disrepair."

"There was unrest among the expelled, a faction attacked the tower's perimeter and managed to damage several of our hothouses before we successfully repelled them," Cassidy improvised using the basic premise of a movie she had watched not long before entering the portal to Tellas. "The resulting food shortage was not welcomed by the workers on the lower levels of the tower. We are not proud of the difficulties we faced, or how we overcame them, but we have kept our tower operating."

"Ah, and your associates, they know of these difficulties?"

"Of course not: they may have suspicions but all they were told was that some equipment failed and we have been sent to obtain replacement parts," Cassidy said, throwing as much scorn into her voice as she could. "The idea of appearing weak to those below us is even more appalling than the idea of requesting aide from our equals. Even telling somebody such as yourself is distasteful, but if such brutish interrogation is the only manner to gain access to the Lord Steward then it is a burden I must bear. Much to the shame of myself and my family."

The chief of security for the Steward Tower bowed formally. "Please forgive my clumsy expression of concern, I assure you that my only concern in the matter is to ensure the safety of the family Steward. Please let us put such unpleasantness behind us and move forward now in our positions as appointed by the council of families and tower staff."

He held the bow until Cassidy said "Very well, I cannot fault you for behaving as I hope our own chief security officers would in similar circumstances."

The chief, seeming to have concluded his investigation to his satisfaction, left the group to finish their tour while he attended to other matters.

CHAPTER TWENTY

After an uneventful afternoon the trio were returned to their rooms. Cassidy settled down with a book about growing papple orchards, a process that seemed to differ very little from growing apples or oranges back on Earth. She noted that Ursula and Sulva were doing a more intense survey of their quarters. Closing the book around her forefinger, she waited for them to finish.

"We do have something very important to discuss," she said once they finished their inspection. "What are we all going to wear to the ball?" The pair stared at her, their faces showing a clear lack of comprehension. "The dance tomorrow night," Cassidy continued. "Surely, we visiting dignitaries cannot appear in this borrowed everyday wear, no matter how comfortable and finely constructed. I didn't think to pack anything suitable for such an event."

Ursula slumped to the floor unceremoniously, a look verging on terror painted on her fine features. "I hadn't given it any thought. I assumed we would wear what they have given us."

"I don't know what the appropriate attire for such an event would be," Sulva apprehensively murmured.

"I usually just wear my uniform to such things, but then again I'm usually only there if I'm working."

The three looked at each other for a minute before rising in unison and rushing off to their respective chambers. Moments later they returned to the main sitting room to compare the garments they had brought with them. Both Ursula and Cassidy had serviceable, if not exactly fashionable dresses which the group agreed could work in anything except the most formal of settings, but Sulva had not thought to bring anything of the sort. As they were sorting through the remaining items, attempting to settle on a choice for the delivery-driver-turned-guard, the serving staff entered with their evening meal.

"Let's ask them," Cassidy said and quickly outlined their current situation.

"We always wear our finest to the gatherings," one of the girls dusting her hands after laying down a tray of bread answered. "I've heard Domina Raigin make arrangements for something to be delivered for your use tomorrow. In your house colours and all, Domina Joplin. And for your staff, not to worry. I'm sure that the hardships of travel must not have been kind to whatever you were carrying with you."

"Well that is both a pleasant surprise and a relief," Cassidy answered.

"Now Winnie, you've gone and ruined Domina Raigin's surprise," the taller server scolded. "Attendance in full regalia is mandatory of course. Lord Steward is scheduled to be there after all."

Before Cassidy could ask how that would affect the dress code, Ursula spoke, "Of course, full respect must be accorded to the high seat of a house. Even from junior members of the other families."

"Well that and the fact that he's almost never seen outside his chambers these days," the first server muttered under her breath, blushing furiously as she realized she had spoken the words aloud. "Oh please, don't tell anybody I said that. It's just he's such a handsome young man and he prefers to spend his time on the upper floors rather than coming down to the lower levels and seeing how things are being run."

"Not that things are run poorly," the older server put in. "It would be nice to see him more than once every three-nine days though. Just to know that the Lord does care how we're all doing."

"The lords are too often busy with other affairs, to monitor all the daily operations," Cassidy said simply. "I'm sure it's just a sign of how hard he's working."

"You kind visitors shouldn't worry yourselves over such matters at any rate. I'm sure your meeting will be arranged in soon," the second server said.

"And I'm sure whatever it is you came here seeking will be dispatched for you to return to the Joplin Tower with. Lord Steward is as generous as he is handsome after all," the first server finished with a blush.

After the pair of servers had left, the group settled down for their meal. They passed the remaining hours of the evening with Sulva and Ursula attempting to teach Cassidy some of the more popular dance steps. Ursula, having spent most of her time in offices and on production floors, only knew one or two of the more common dance routines performed at such gatherings. Sulva, on the other hand, was a veritable treasure trove.

The former delivery driver walked them through a number of styles similar to many Cassidy had seen in movies and plays, including a solo sequence that seemed to blend tap dancing, line dancing, and what she thought of as traditional highland dancing. At the end of the lesson Sulva told them, "Hopefully the dances will be of the easier sort without the pomp of the higher forms, there just isn't enough time to teach them to you properly."

Cassidy, flushed with exertion, grinned sheepishly, "Perhaps I'll sprain an ankle to save you the embarrassment of seeing your student flub the steps."

"That might be for the best," Ursula spoke from a nearby chair where she was rubbing her feet. "It might save the toes of whoever is fool enough to ask you to dance."

With that the group went to bed.

In the morning they awoke to find three packages neatly wrapped in a pulpy-looking off-white paper that reminded Cassidy of newspaper. A note pinned to the top of the packages read simply:

To: Joplin Delegates,
For tonight. Please ensure the fit is correct before our scheduled tour,
Barbara Shrub

"Who's Barbara Shrub?" Sulva asked of nobody in particular as they opened the packages. Each contained elegant fringed dresses in the silver and purple of House Joplin. The smallest dress, clearly meant for Cassidy, was of a silver silk accented with purple sequins, with fringes that alternated a royal purple so deep as to seem black and silver. The other two dresses were plain black with the same silver and black patterning to the fringe-work. The two Tellans seemed scandalized by the low-cut neck-lines and high hems on the skirts. Cassidy thought them rather conservative but fun enough, something she could wear to pub night at a conference. Each dress was accompanied by a pair of soft slippers—thick silken socks really, that stretched to fit the wearer's foot. "Dancing in those might really sprain my ankle," Cassidy told her friends as she examined the footwear.

"They allow you to pivot and twirl as you dance," Sulva explained. "There's a gripping pattern of tree sap thread woven through them that will provide extra traction while allowing for freedom of movement. They've been the standard footwear for dancing for years."

At Cassidy's dubiousness Ursula told her, "Just try them on, you'll see that they are more than sufficient for interior wear, and should fit comfortably under your normal footwear. Let's try these frocks on and see if the local seamstresses are better than those we're used to."

The trio made their way into their separate rooms. Once alone, Cassidy was relieved to find that she wouldn't need any help to don the dress since it was designed to be fastened by the wearer. As she closed the small buttons, she noted that it was a little loose but was quite comfortable and, upon examining herself in the mirror, looked better on than it had in the box. The colours complemented her hair and her lightly tanned skin in a way that she was more than a little satisfied to see. As she pulled on the dancing slippers, she decided that she quite liked the full effect of the ensemble. She did a quick walking test of the slippers and found the mixture of tractions provided by the gripping pattern—which ranged from a very firm grip to absolutely no grip—an odd combination, but hopefully she would learn how to walk in them at least before the ball that evening.

As she emerged from her chamber, she saw her companions already waiting for her. They simply stood for a moment, staring at each other. Cassidy felt like she had only seen her new friends as caterpillars but the joy on their faces in their borrowed finery revealed them as jewelled butterflies. After a quick study of them she was relieved to see that the looseness seemed to be more a fashion of the world than a failure on the part of their seamstress. They each did quick turns for the others in turn and agreed that the frocks would do for whatever the Steward Tower might hold for them, especially once Cassidy took the time to master her new shoes.

Nancy stopped by, informing them that with the upcoming festivities they would be given the day to themselves in order to better prepare themselves for the evening, and that they should take the available time to rest. When she returned, the trio were ready for the event. The small group made their way through the corridors in excited silence, the faint echoes of music drawing them in the lavishly decorated hallways that led them to ball.

The room was filled to capacity with only those performing essential tasks in absentia. Each attendee was announced via the public address system as they entered while the musicians played a piece that reminded Cassidy of slow summer days spent in the sun. All heads turned when the Joplin party was announced, everybody curious to see the visitors from out of tower.

They made their way into the room, sipping drinks handed to them by a server in the tower colours, exchanging pleasantries with any who approached them, as Nancy took them to their assigned table. They were seated within sight of the Lord Steward's table, well out of conversational range, yet still in a position of prominence. It did not matter since the Lord's seat sat empty. A meal, noticeably smaller than that which they typically received in their rooms was served as they sat, with Nancy urging them all to eat before the dancing began in earnest.

The trio watched as the band moved effortlessly from one song to the next. The Steward Tower residents moved through dance routines that involved both rounds and single partners, Sulva rising to join after the third dance, with Ursula joining the steps at the start of the next song. Cassidy sipped a glass of papple juice, the only thing being served at the tables, and watched the intricate steps as the dancers circled the floor counter-clockwise.

"I would have thought that a daughter from the Joplin Tower would know the steps to all the popular dances," a man in simple green and red plaid said to her.

"Sadly no," she responded. "My education covered many topics, but formal dancing was left for my more agile siblings. I can manage simple steps but very little else."

The figure gestured at a chair, seating himself at Cassidy's nod. "So, a solitary observer from one of the larger towers comes to my tower and doesn't recognize the man she has been sent to meet?" he asked. "Or should I say a solitary observer and her carefully selected team of escorts?"

Cassidy blushed and nearly rose to bow to Lord Steward before she caught herself. Gripping the seat of her chair with the hand not holding her glass she responded, "Forgive me, Lord Steward, between the lighting in here and the fact that we have been here for nearly a week and you have not found time to meet with me, I simply didn't realize it was you."

The surprise on his face was too plain to be an act. "You've been here how long? I was told you arrived yesterday and requested the evening to recover from the hardships of your journey," he stammered.

She sipped her drink, taking a moment to study how he sat like she would a student who had come to her asking for an extension on a paper. "We came seeking parts for some malfunctioning equipment in the Joplin Tower and have been here for more than seven days and have requested meetings with you each day since our arrival," she told him flatly. "Each day we were told you were busy but could possibly see us the next day."

He lounged back in his seat with a long sigh and reached for one of the glasses at the table. "You are the youngest Joplin, are you not?" At her nod he continued. "I too was the youngest and never meant to take control of the tower. Like you, my family would send me on errands to fetch and carry and deliver messages, missions just like this, until my brothers fell ill. Now the staff keeps me in the dark and makes proclamations in my name. Which is fine, everything is functioning just as it should. I'm surprised I managed to sneak away from them tonight but I guess the extra scrutiny placed on your companions made them relax their vigilance on me."

Cassidy choked on her drink a little at this.

"Oh, you didn't know, I'm little more than a prisoner here," he sipped his papple juice and made a face. "True I'm kept in all the luxury we can manage here but I'm only trotted out at formal occasions and have little say in anything that happens here at all. If you want your parts, or whatever it is you were sent here for, you'll have to get it yourself and make your way out of here. If you could bring me out too, I'd be ever so pleased."

"You want me to take you out into the frozen wastelands your parents have made this region?" she blurted.

"Ah but your family has done it too Domina Joplin. Your hands are every bit as filthy as mine, despite us both being the expendable children," he sighed as he emptied his glass. "I wish they were serving some sort of brandy at this event, perhaps later. But I digress, I do see the things being done in my name and despise them. If I had the freedom, I'd shut the tower down. It might only affect the nearby region, but surely with the loss of a thirteenth of the influence the other towers might struggle to maintain the mess we've managed to create. Ah, I believe I see some of my security team approaching."

With a nod over her shoulder to confirm his words, he leaned across the table, as if attempting to better hear her words. He managed to lay a hand on her upper thigh as Chapel placed a hand on the Lord's shoulder. "Lord Steward, there you are," the security chief said. "I see you have made the acquaintance of Domina Joplin. Unfortunately, its time for you to address the tower. I've your speech right here. I'm sure the Joplin emissary will excuse us."

As the pair made their way towards the stage Cassidy noted the rough way in which the chief handled the young Lord Steward, though the security officer made it look like assisting a drunk on his way. As the pair reached the stage the crowd paused wherever they were and turned to face the dais. Cassidy shifted her weight and felt something slide along the smooth fabric of her skirt. Looking down, she found an envelope which she quickly slid into the top of her socklet, disguising the motion as simply adjusting the garment.

The speech the Lord gave was full of the expected pleasantries: production was up, the weather was behaving properly, the people outside the tower were starting to see reason and would soon perform their part in the great planetary order of families. Through it all Chapel stood beside Lord Steward, a reptilian smile on his face and satisfaction in his eyes. The Lord concluded by formally welcoming the Joplin delegation to the tower and asking everybody to enjoy the rest of their evening.

As the Lord left the dais to rousing applause Chapel gestured to the band, who struck up a lively rock-a-billy-esque tune that set Cassidy's toes to tapping. It was with a certain relief that she saw that the formalized sequence dances were concluded for the evening, to be replaced with a free flowing form of movement that reminded her of the common steps seen in bars and at house parties, wherever people felt the rhythm of a good beat.

Ursula returned to the table with a pair of glasses in her hand. "That was the Lord Steward I saw you speaking with, wasn't it?" she asked.

Cassidy took the glass from the engineer, sipped it, then replied, "Yes, and it is not a conversation for us to have here."

"Really?" Ursula asked archly.

"Yes," Cassidy replied, annoyance plain in her voice. "Is it too early for visiting dignitaries to duck out yet?"

She was cut off by a tap on her shoulder. Turning, she saw a trio of the garden guards with sheepish smiles, "Would you ladies like to dance?"

And Cassidy danced with the guard, with an engineer, with a chef, with servers. She danced until the band started to pack their instruments away and Nancy ushered her and her friends back to their rooms. As they began to settle in for the evening Cassidy told them of her brief meeting with the entrapped Lord before climbing into her bed fully clothed and promptly falling into a deep slumber.

CHAPTER TWENTY ONE

Cassidy was surprised to awaken in the early hours of the morning feeling so well rested, almost as surprised as she was to find herself still dressed from the night before. She made her way to the wash chamber where she indulged herself in a hot shower, luxuriating in the steamy stream of water in a way she hadn't for months back on Earth. She felt like she was at the end of a field season and taking advantage of the facilities before she'd return home and have to take responsibility for the bills again.

Feeling as relaxed and clean as she had after her first shower in the tower, she wrapped herself in towels, collected her dirty clothing, and made her way back to the bed chamber. As she sorted the dirty clothing, she rediscovered the note from Lord Steward tucked into the socklet. Amazed that she could have forgotten something that must have been important for the prisoner Lord to take such a risk to deliver to her. Opening the envelope, she was surprised and a little disappointed to discover that the message consisted of a string of numbers and a crudely sketched map.

She quickly dressed and made a quick search of their

shared suite for Ursula and Sulva. She found the pair in the sitting area down the hall from their suite proper.

"You're finally awake," Ursula exclaimed as Cassidy seated herself at the table.

"Thank you for letting me sleep, I needed it," Cassidy said with a smile, pouring herself a cup from the teapot on the table. "I found this and I'm not sure I can make any sense of it."

Sulva took the document and quickly looked it over. "It's a duty schedule. I hope whoever lost it won't miss their shift start," she said quietly and reached to turn on the radionic. "Specifically, it's the duty schedule for the tower control centre and a map through the air ducts to get into it."

Ursula took the missive with the inquiry, "Where did you get this?"

Cassidy placed her tea aside and said, "It fell into my lap, literally. Lord Steward dropped it there as they took him away. He seemed to be fully aware that his staff were giving us the runaround but wanted to help. He thinks the whole permanent winter thing is wrong and wants it to end. At least that's the impression I got from him when we spoke."

Sulva grunted, "From what you've said he's little more than a prisoner. Kept on so the residents don't realize that Chapel is actually in charge. You said he actually asked you to shut down the network?"

Cassidy took a deep breath before saying, "Yes, he asked it as one fourth child to another."

Ursula smacked her forehead with her right hand, "Of course he did, I forgot all about the accident just before the towers were vitalized. Three of the four Steward children were killed when a portion of the tower collapsed on them during a tour of the construction. There was a huge investigation made by the guardians but they determined that there was no wrong-doing, simply a fault in one of the beams that had not been seen during the construction. Although that didn't stop the rumour mongers from repeating all sorts of imprecations against the Lady Steward."

"I remember that," Sulva cut in. "It wasn't until after a few similar incidents had occurred at other buildsites here in the Aetalus that those rumours died down. Though among some of the guardians and private security forces people claimed that the other accidents might have been the Lady's doing as well. She had expressed doubts about if it was wise to tamper with the weather to such an extreme and some thought she'd committed the sabotage but accidentally killed both of her daughters and one of her sons."

"That must be why she disappeared from the social circuits in the time before they vitalized the towers," Ursula concluded for the trio with the tones of a detective in a television melodrama. "Not just the loss of the majority of her family, but also the guilt of having killed them with her actions."

Cassidy shook her head at the deluge of Steward family history, which seemed to have played out in the local news like some kind of radio drama for the residents. "Will any of that help us get into the control room? Beyond it maybe explaining why the Lord Steward is willing to throw us this huge assist?"

"By all accounts, any of the families with a fourth child just let that child grow more or less wild, at least by their normal structures. That's why we chose for you to impersonate a fourth. They're known to be eccentric," Ursula said. "The Steward fourth was little known before the accident, though it was said he favoured his mother's politics. I think everybody just assumed that with the death of his siblings he'd taken on the mantle of head of the family willingly."

"You mean people thought that his stance was posturing, designed to get attention?" Cassidy asked. "Like everybody seemed to assume that Cassidy Joplin's studies were an effort to stay out of the papers?"

Sulva sipped at her tea for a moment before she replied, "Yes, exactly like that. A face not meant to draw attention with no regard of what might be behind it."

"I guess we do whatever it is they have planned for us and try to get in on the next day the plan says we can," Cassidy said. "When is the next time that the roster should be right?"

Ursula folded the document into her pocket and said, "Two days from now. It feels as though we've wasted so much of our time here already."

The others nodded in agreement.

"I'll make sure I'm ready," Cassidy began as she stood.

"Us too," Ursula chirped excitedly.

Sulva shook her head, "It might be best if only one of us go. And I think we all know who it has to be."

"Me, of course," both Cassidy and Ursula spoke, then looked at the flat disapproval on the face of the former delivery driver.

"If the Joplin emissary disappears for a time it will cause concern. Likewise, for the engineer," Sulva began adopting a tone that brooked no argument. "The only one of us who won't be missed is the transport officer, the glorified guard, and that means I have to do it. I'll take whatever advice you can give me, but we all know it's an operation for one."

"Adopting the role you were thrust into, is that it?" Ursula asked.

"No, she's just thinking further ahead than we are," Cassidy replied. "And she's right. The Steward staff will take note if you or I go missing for any amount of time, but if our guard goes missing, they'll just assume that I gave my servant some time off. Makes no difference that Sulva isn't actually staff as they see it, that's how they see the three of us."

"But neither of you would know how to adjust the tower controls," Ursula said urgently. "You haven't studied the mechanisms and might not be able to follow the procedures properly."

"Then you will make sure to write out the step-by-step procedure for her," Cassidy said with a sigh. "I don't like having to sit back and do nothing, but it has to be her. We'll arrange for us to have a meal with the security chief or something and say Sulva felt ill or just wanted the evening off. I assume that it works that way here too anyway, people aren't expected to work all the time."

Cassidy drifted about their floor, casually looking at the books they had been provided, checking the doors of the other suites and finding most of them locked. When she found one that was open, she went inside. The suite was almost identical to their own, just as she had expected. The floor was set aside as a guest accommodation for visiting dignitaries of a certain station, after all. With couches and chairs to sit on, tables to work and eat from. Basic structures repeating across the floor, echoing through the levels, with variations to suit the time. Like a game of telephone or rumour played out in the levels of the tower and across the dimensions. She sat in one of the chairs near the window, looking out at the community from this new side of the tower, seeing it from this new angle.

In the street below she saw the snow piled to the second-floor windows of the vacant building across the street. Beyond that first line of buildings she saw smaller structures, visible only as corners poking through the crust of snow. Some of the roadways, now little more than troughs in the snow revealed by nothing more than the shadows caught in the depression caused by the passage of those left outside the tower.

The plan seemed foolish to her: freeze a world to extort money from it. Force them into small groups and deny them all the comforts their society could provide, based on nothing more than the greed of those in power. The human experience echoed and distorted again on the inter-dimensional scale. But what if they could change that here? What if disabling this tower could be the spark that started the fire of societal advancement, freeing at least this small corner of the world from the yoke of oppressors? She was tired and longed for the comfort of her own bed, even with the worries that awaited her at home. The bills piling higher than the snow outside, not knowing if her contract would be renewed next semester, the yearly scramble for grants to continue her excavations. She rested her chin in her hands and watched as the snow began falling, again.

It was dark when she rose from the chair, stiff from having dozed off sitting up. Slowly she made her way to their chambers and found her companions just starting their evening meal. She ate with them silently as they discussed the procedure to disable the weather device. She excused herself from the table and went to her bed. Once she was sure her companions had retired to their own chambers—when had it become their new normal to sleep in their own beds, she wondered—she put her bag over her shoulder and left the suites.

CHAPTER TWENTY TWO

Cassidy made her way through the darkened corridors to the unlocked suite she had found earlier that day. Once inside, she locked the door behind her and pulled the cover from an air duct, took a deep breath, and climbed in.

The ducts were bigger than they would have been on Earth but still a tight fit for her. Slowly she made her way through the hot air in the ductwork, in the light of a flashlight, towards the nearest vertical shaft she could find. Once there she saw somebody had scrawled the words "Gym, Guests, Laundry" on the wall in descending order and, hoping that this would be the case at every floor, she began to climb. Her footfalls echoing on the ladder, she paused on the next floor to remove her shoes in favour of the socklets she wore underneath and shed her outer coat, then resumed her climb. She passed words which read "Office, Accountants, Repair, Residence" before she finally reached a floor labelled "Mech and Con" in the same inky scrawl.

She climbed onto the nearest ledge, extinguishing her flashlight once she was settled. She lay flat with her eyes closed, allowing herself a moment to both catch her breath and let her eyes adjust to the dim light in the ducts. In truth the light did little more than allow her to see which vents opened on lit areas, which were the most likely areas to be occupied. She checked her map, straining to make out some of the detail on the paper and failing, she moved towards the nearest light source as quietly as she could.

She was within a meter of the nearest vent, eyes focused on her goal, when a pair of boots stopped on the other side of the slatted opening. Cassidy held her breath, wishing the boots to move on. She watched as a hand came into view, opening the louvres a little. Making herself as small as possible, she turned her face to the floor; it wasn't until she heard the boots move on that she exhaled and looked up again. She took a further count of thirty before she continued her approach to the now wide-open vent.

All that she could see through the slats was a corridor. Nothing was visible from her floor-level vantage point to indicate where on the level she might be. Quickly she pulled out the map and attempted to puzzle out where she might be on it, an exercise that proved futile. The sketch gave her little information beyond the control room. Sighing, Cassidy pulled the louvres closed and turned back toward the upright shaft. She treated as she had been told to treat mazes as a child, and using the shaft where she had entered as her starting point, she took every right turning where she could see a light. She found many openings on corridors, and some on offices, when she found herself at a broom closet, she took the opportunity to step in and stretch.

As she breathed the cleanser-perfumed air, she reflected that she really had no idea what she was doing;

she was no technician trained to operate anything more complicated than her phone, but given that they relied on transistor tubes here the controls couldn't be much more complicated than her phone anyway. Besides, every piece of equipment will break if you try hard enough—hadn't she seen proof of that on every dig she'd taken part in? Taking a deep breath, she pressed her ear to the closet door; hearing nothing, she opened the door a crack and risked a peek at the hall and was delighted to find she was actually at the starting point indicated on her map. Pulling the door closed behind her, she did a few more quick stretches, then climbed back into the ventilation shafts and followed the path laid out for her.

She peered through the grating at the underside of several desks and saw three booted feet. At least two people in the control room, but there was no noise of human activity. The tubes hummed with their stored charges, the ventilation whispered around her, and a clock ticked in the room before her. Gently she grasped the grating before her and began to ease it free from the wall. With agonizing slowness, she forced it free, millimetre by silent millimetre, until her shoulders throbbed with the strain. When it came free of the housing, unexpectedly quicker than she anticipated, she nearly dropped the piece of metal to the floor. Instead she managed to hold it while debating her next move.

After what felt like hours of watching the boots not move, a high warbling sound rang through the tower. The booted feet sprang up. "Fire alarm," a woman's voice said. "Make sure the auto is on and let's get out of here." The walking of boots followed by the sound of the closing door was the only response.

Cassidy wasted no time and crawled from the cramped vent. Immediately she crossed to the door and locked it. Next, she turned to the control panel. She had expected a large computer but what she saw before her staggered her. The device hulked against the wall like something from a 1940s sci-fi movie, almost as big as a moving van, covered in knobs and dials and flashing lights. Close inspection revealed that everything had been labelled at one point but whatever material they had used to make those labels was worn away with use. Here she could make out a letter, there part of a word, but nowhere was there anything to indicate what the controls did. She tried her best to remember the instructions Ursula had given to Sulva in order to reset the machine and shut it down, but even if she could recall them, she wouldn't have been able to find the controls needed with the incomplete labels. Taking a deep breath, she reached out with her right hand and did the only thing that made sense to her: she simple flipped all the switches. Every knob that was dialed clockwise, she dialed counter-clockwise. If a switch was in the up position, she flipped it down. Where possible, she broke the control as she went, snapping the dials from potentiometers and cracking the levers on switches. Seeing nothing else to tamper with, Cassidy grabbed one of the chairs, raised it above her head and brought it down on the console repeatedly. Feeling that her task was accomplished, Cassidy took a step back to survey her work.

Realizing all had gone still, Cassidy crawled back into the ventilation shafts, pulled the grating in behind her, and scurried into the darkness. She had had almost made her way back to the cleaning closet when she heard a new alarm begin to sound. Adrenaline pumping now, she attempted to retrace her path through the vents. At the first vertical shaft she came to she headed down; checking the legend scrawled on each floor as she descended, she made her way as swiftly and silently as possible.

With each floor she descended the ventilation system grew lighter as the levels were lit. Frantically, she searched for the items she had abandoned on her travels as she drew closer to her destination. Finally, she found her boots and outer wear and stuffed them into her bag as she emerged into the empty suite where she had begun her journey. Taking a moment to tidy up, she let her hair down and entered the chaos of the hallway.

The corridor was in chaos; crowded with security personnel, serving staff, and people in tower uniforms Cassidy didn't recognize, all pushing against one another. All shouting at each other. It was into this tumult she was drawn as the door of the suite closed itself behind her. With no other choice, she tried to ride the flow of the crowd towards the suite she shared with Sulva and Ursula. She had just entered the crowd when she felt herself being grabbed from behind and hands attempting to pull her from the crush of people.

Struggling against the unknown assailant, she lunged into the crowd, straight into the back of one of the security personnel. The guard spun around and reached for her. Cassidy ducked beneath the taller man's grasp, thankful for her shorter stature on this world and began weaving her way deeper into the crowd seeking what she hoped would be the safety of her rooms. She was nearly there when she heard cries of "Get her!" erupt behind her.

A surge of the crowd sent her crashing into a door. Feeling the pressure build behind her, she took a blow to the back of her head as she grabbed the doorknob and twisted, feeling momentary relief as the door opened followed by immediate panic as more hands took hold of her and pulled her deeper into the room while other hands closed and secured the door behind her.

Cassidy lay facedown on the floor where she had been dropped, gasping for air. With what seemed to be the last of her strength, she forced herself to roll onto her back and found herself looking up into the faces of her best friends on this planet before she blacked out.

CHAPTER TWENTY THREE

Cassidy had no idea how much time had passed when she awoke, the sounds of a thunder storm raging outside the window of her darkened room.

"Finally awake?" Ursula's familiar voice came from just outside her door. "I was going to ask where you went, but I think we've figured that out by now."

"I got tired of waiting and might have done something rash," Cassidy gave a rueful smile.

"Well from what we've been able to put together it was a good thing that you did decide to do something rash," Sulva said as she walked into the room with a cup of tea. "You heard the alarms, I take it? Apparently, there was a dispute between a group of engineers and the security team."

Cassidy gasped, "I thought it was a fire alarm."

"It was; one of the engineers pulled it during the ballyhoo from what I've been told," Ursula interjected. "When we heard the alarm and found your bed empty, we were afraid that it might have something to do with you, but on our way down the stairs we ran into one of the ladies who usually brings our meals and she told us."

"Under no circumstances are you to leave your floor tonight," Sulva cut in with a passable imitation of the red-headed server they had chatted with many times. "She had seen the fighting and was on her way up to warn us to stay clear. I think she was hoping that we'd give her shelter too. She's asleep on the couch by the way."

"When she discovered that you weren't actually in our suite, she figured that you'd gone to visit somebody special; I think she was hoping it was the Lord Steward in all honest. For the most part nobody tried our door through all the fighting, they gathered on this floor because it divides the upper and lower castes' residences," Ursula paused. "We kept hoping you'd come by sooner or later."

"When I heard the shouting in the corridor change, I decided to see what had happened," Sulva said. "By the time I worked up the courage to take a look you had made it to the door and fell in when I opened it. If Ursula hadn't acted so quickly then I'd never have gotten the door closed again.

Head spinning, Cassidy pulled herself out of bed. It took her a moment to realize that the thunderous noise was coming from outside the building as well as the noises from the corridor. "Did it work?" she asked, turning toward the nearest window. "Did I shut down the tower?"

Looking at the rain lashing the window and the lightning arcing through the sky was all the answer she needed. "Storms were predicted as a potential side effect of a tower failing," Ursula said smoothly. "If the system can be brought back online then complete control can be resumed. If this one remains incapacitated then the others should fail within days and natural weather patterns resume. It looks like you did it, yes."

The three stood at the window for a moment, watching the play of lightning in the dark sky as the pounding from the corridor grew louder and louder until the door came crashing into the room followed by a quartet of the engineers and labourers.

"Oh, good, you're all in here," the Lord Steward said from the rear of the group. "There's been a bit of bother tonight and, long story short, the security forces have all been locked away. Also, somebody has wreaked absolute havoc on the weather manipulator but that's a by-the-by sort of thing since I was going to shut it down anyway. Now, Cassidy not Joplin, mind telling me what your role in all this was?"

CHAPTER TWENTY FOUR

Lightning flashed behind the trio and thunder rumbled through the night before Cassidy responded with, "You knew? You knew and didn't say anything?"

The Lord of Steward Tower spoke through giggles, "Of course I knew. I met Cassidy Joplin at boarding school years ago. Even carried somewhat of a torch for her, though she never had any interest in dating one of her students. You're at least five years too young and perhaps half a meter too short. I'm impressed that you fooled Chapel; I might have believed you if I didn't know her personally."

"Then why not reveal her?" Sulva asked. "All of us for that matter?"

"Well there was the whole thing about me being a prisoner in my own home," he chirped. "Besides, the whole not wanting to be an evil overlord so much. I was hoping you lot would be my key to freedom. And, if I'm being completely honest with everybody, I was bored."

Those gathered in the room stared at him dumbstruck. "You were bored! With everything that's going on in the world around you. Everything that's happening in

Aetalus. Everything that's gone on in your tower. You let a bunch of outsiders do what they pleased because you were bored?" Cassidy took a deep breath and slapped the Lord Steward as hard as she could across the face. "You let yourself be locked away and used as a figurehead: did it not once occur to you that you could have been doing something to help the people who had allowed your family such control?"

Grinning behind the hand currently rubbing his cheek, "I suppose convincing the engineers to help me oust the security forces that held me prisoner might have been a little self-serving, but it was also the easiest way to take back control of the tower. And let's not forget passing information to you as well—that was neither easily arranged or entirely for my own good. But you still haven't answered my question: who are you really and why are you here?"

"I'm a traveller from another world sent here to find whatever any useful technology my home planet could benefit from," she said calmly. "I entered your realm through a portal from my own."

He sat heavily on the floor "Are you truly from beyond the portals? They were only emerging when, well, when my family and the others started to freeze those refusing to pay the scandalous rates the families expected. So at least one does lead somewhere habitable: all those who had entered them had failed to return."

'The portal worlds have portal worlds,' Cassidy thought, then quickly pushed the idea down. "I need a copy of the plans for the weather control centres and then I need to make my way home," she said in the calmest voice she could muster. "I've been away for too long as it is and must get back to where I belong."

Sulva spoke up from nearby, "I'll help you get wherever you need to go, Cassidy, but we'll need to wait for the weather to calm a bit."

"No, I've been here too long as it is," the frustration in Cassidy's voice plain. "I need to go home, I need to tell the professor about the other portals here, I need to sleep in my own bed, I need to get back to my normal life, what's left of it anyway. Get me a copy of the plans and let me go home as quick as I can."

Quickly she went about the room gathering her belongings and stuffing them into her messenger bag. "I've got a rough idea of where I came through in relation to the first shelter we were in and—"

"And you will sit down and have something to eat," Ursula said, thunder punctuating her words. "If the rains cause the snow to melt, we'll all be stuck in this tower for at least a few days. I'll find you a copy of the plans if you're sure you still want them, but nobody will be going anywhere in this mess."

"If only we had some sort of device that could stop the rain, or at least allow us to slow it's falling," the Lord mused quietly. "We'll offer whatever assistance we can, when travel is possible, but given the abrupt shift from controlled weather to being the only pocket of natural climatic activity, that will be at least a few days. Settle in here. We'll monitor the outside and keep you informed of the situation as it develops."

Cassidy shuffled to the window, watching the lightning play across the skyline as the snows melted, revealing the streets beneath.

CHAPTER TWENTY FIVE

Six days passed, by the count of the clock, the sky had begun to lighten. Six days of discussing the places she had seen through other portals. Six days of staring out the window as the snow became water that flooded first the streets and then the buildings. Six days of watching people seek shelter on the higher floors of buildings until their own nearly deserted floor had seen all the rooms filled to capacity. Six days after she had demolished the weather control device, Cassidy saw the sun in the sky once more.

"I've arranged for a dory to take us to the portal," Sulva told her. "Hopefully you'll be able to make your way through and return to your homeland."

Cassidy thanked all those present as she collected her belongings. Anxious to be off, she left a note with Ursula explaining how to contact her or the professor should either ever make their way to Earth, then made her way to the waiting boat with Sulva.

As the pair rowed down the roadways she marvelled at the submerged buildings. Here a roof just broke the surface, there a full floor of a structure could be seen. In most cases structures were only revealed by ripples in the stagnating waters that covered them. Occasionally they saw people waving through windows and from exposed rooftops, but mostly the voyage was little more than stroking the oars.

As the sun began to set, Cassidy fished out her portal locator and began to scan the area where she thought the portal was. As the device began its pinging, they steered towards a mountain on the outskirts of the community; it seemed much shorter in the flood waters than her downward trajectory during the snowstorm had led her to believe. The pair circled, looking for some point of entry. Cassidy couldn't believe her luck when she saw some of the symbols she had marked at the mouth of the cave where she had first entered this world. True the water would be nearly to her hips when she entered the hollow, but finally her home was in sight.

Sulva sat in the small craft outside the cavern until she saw a flash of light, and waited a little longer until she was certain that her strange friend from another reality had gone. The she turned her small craft and headed back to the community they had freed together.

Cassidy stepped through the other side of the portal and pulled her phone from her pocket, only remembering at the last moment that she hadn't charged it in days. Time to make her way back to the office again.

A few days later, back in her own clothes and with a fresh haircut, she entered the office of Professor Gamgee. "I can't keep haring off on whatever new quest you've come up with for me," she began. "Sure, side missions are great in video games, but I've got bills and rent and a main story-line for my life to consider."

The professor looked up from his tablet, keyed the display off and placed it facedown on the table before him.

"When I left, I was looking at a performance review to explain my abscesses from teaching and a pile of bills that I could barely afford even if I hadn't missed any work," she told him. "I love the work you give me, but I need to survive too."

"I was thinking you needed a salary," he told her calmly. "A salary, an expense account, and perhaps a gratuity for items retrieved. To be quite honest, I have been concerned about your divided focus, even without the added pressure you receive from the department to recruit more archaeologists."

She looked at him with stunned silence.

The professor continued, "Very well, you will be compensated for your lodgings as well, but that is all I can manage at this time. My research grants are large but are still limited for all of that. Is that agreeable?"

Cassidy, unable to fully articulate her thoughts gushed "Yes, thank you, oh my goodness that'd be great."

The professor nodded curtly and pointed towards the nearest empty table top, "Now let's see what you found."

ACKNOWLEDGEMENTS

The authors would like to pay special thanks to the *Slipstreamers* committee at Engen Books, including Amanda Labonté, Matthew LeDrew, AJ Ryan, Ellen Curtis, Erin Vance, and, Lauralana Dunne.

Without their tireless efforts, none of this would have been possible.

Special thanks to this episode's editor, Ali House.

Shannon K Green would also like to thank Beverley and Clifford Green for their constant support; Bronwynn Erskine for being a patient and sometimes useful sounding board; and, most importantly, Dr. Lisa M. Daly for reminding him when to use which punctuation marks, how to make to make the words flow, and for making sure he did the little things like eating and bathing when the process got difficult.

ABOUT THE AUTHOR

A gifted author with a talent for the strange, **Shannon K Green** has been recognized in both the genre community and the contemporary literary community for his pursuits. In the past, he has been shortlisted for the 1996 Arts and Letters Award, and later won the 2015 Audience Choice Steampunk Newfoundland Showcase.

Green's short fiction has appeared in *Fantasy from the Rock, The Hamthology, Jibbernocky* and the bestselling collections *Chillers from the Rock, Dystopia from the Rock, Flights from the Rock, Pulp Science-Fiction from the Rock, From the Rock Stars* and, this year, *in Mythology from the Rock.*

JD Ryot is the reclusive creator of the *Slipstreamers* series from Engen Books. JD is an avid fan of young adult literature and adventure serials. When asked if they had come to this world through a portal themselves, JD Ryot refused to answer. No record of their birth has ever been found... on this world.

www.ingramcontent.com/pod-product-compliance
Lightning Source LLC
Chambersburg PA
CBHW051954170626
46808CB00007B/2608